Elemental Stalking

Welcome to Freyshire: Book 1

Jen Drapp

Chapter 1

I wasn't a stalker.

If someone saw me right now staring out the window, it may have looked like that, but seriously. Was it wrong to just casually "people watch"? Then, maybe, find one person to focus on and casually watch that *particular* person? A little bit more closely? And a little more often?

Okay, it really did sound a lot like stalking.

I couldn't help it though. I mean, what else was one supposed to do behind the veil? Besides, it was only for one night a month. So...it wasn't true stalking.

"Stalk much, Calina?"

I jerked my head around and gave Shani my best 'are you reading my mind' face, tilting my head and raising my eyebrow.

"Are you listening to my thoughts again?" I hated when she did that.

She rolled her gorgeous brown eyes. "I didn't need to. I know exactly what you're staring at. Or *who*, I should say." The corners of her mouth curved up into a slight smirk as she came over to the window and peered over my shoulder.

"I'm sure I have no idea what you're talking about," I lied. But I didn't budge from my spot at the window. It was a hazy view, looking from one realm to another, but after some practice, it wasn't impossible to see the world of the living from the world of the dead.

Out beyond the veil on the outskirts of the town of Freyshire, lay a tiny cottage. It looked like every other cottage in the old village nestled comfortably above the dark valley. One-story, timber-framed, and surrounded by cobblestone paths that connected to the neighboring homes and the main road that led into town. So, what made this particular cottage stare-worthy?

Shani was right. It was not a what, but a *who*. And I had no idea who he was. But, for some reason he caught my eye a couple of full moons ago, and I'd stalked...I mean, *noticed* him since. Every time that I saw him, he was sitting on the back porch in a white Adirondack chair, dark brown and wavy hair a mess, engrossed in a book that he read by the firelight of a nearby lantern.

I'm not sure what it was about him that made me want to keep seeing him. Yes, he was cute and looked to be about my age, but there was something else. Maybe that's why I looked for him each time I came behind the veil. Every full moon, that is, as that's the only time my dad invited me here. I think I was hoping to someday solve the puzzle that was this random person. This beautiful human, no less.

Or maybe I was just a stalker.

"He is super cute. Have you gone into town to see if he actually exists?" Shani laughed and nudged me, before resting her chin on my shoulder.

Shani was my best friend. I'd known her since we were both in diapers and she frequently came to my dad's place with me. To anyone else, it may have been a little awkward spending the night behind the veil that separates the world of the living from the dead. But what could I say? Shani loved the weirdness and oddly enough, even loved my dad. It didn't faze her at all that he was the Erlking and liked to go on wild hunts once a month with armies of dead guys. Not even in the slightest. I think she secretly wanted to go on a hunt with him one day and hoped he might invite her if she hung out at his place often enough.

Oh yeah, Shani was one of Set's daughters. Like, the Egyptian god of chaos, Set. Right. *That* Set. So, I supposed that she was used to supernatural beings and all-around terrifying dads. The two of us were basically joined at the hip since birth, and she knew pretty much everything about me. Even the stuff I've told to my therapist. In hindsight, I probably should've fired the therapist and just talked to Shani. It would have been cheaper.

"I'm sure he goes to school...works..." Shani lifted her chin and shrugged. "We could go into Freyshire, and you could take your stalking to a whole new level. See him every day instead of once a month."

That was an idea.

I sighed suddenly wishing that I had put off going to the Academy for a semester. "We have to be at the Academy tomorrow for orientation, remember? Going to the village will have to wait until next weekend." *Or never*, I thought.

Shani and I were leaving for our first semester of college the next day. She seemed super excited about going and being my roommate. I, on the other hand, had mixed feelings.

Especially since her half-sister, Reema, was also going to be rooming with us.

"Deal."

"Wait, what?" I broke my stare down with the mystery boy and turned on my friend. She was now sitting on my bed, scrolling through her phone.

She looked up at me innocently, flashing me her huge smile that she used on her father whenever she wanted something. "Next weekend we'll go on a search mission for your mystery man." She nodded then went back to her screen.

"No, Shani, I was kidding. I mean, we can go into town to hang out next weekend but I'm not going on a man hunt." I stared at her for a minute. "Shani? Ok? It was just a joke."

"Whatever you say." She pursed her lips but didn't look at me.

I shook my head in frustration. Ugh, she could be so difficult sometimes. "Come on, we should get our stuff together for tomorrow and try to get some sleep. Sunrise will be here before we know it."

Shani jumped up from the bed in excitement and paced around the room, going on and on about all of the fun and crazy things we were going to do in college.

It was like the last conversation had never happened.

I tossed a couple of framed pictures of me and my parents into a box and grabbed the few remaining clothing items from my dresser, folding them neatly into my suitcase. I didn't have that much stuff at my dad's, but I still was a bit nostalgic as I went through the things that I was planning on taking with me.

I looked around the dusty old chamber that my father had transformed into a little girl's bedroom. Though the walls were gray brick like the rest of the castle, the tiny pink and purple fairy lights that lined the ceiling, made it feel brighter. He had one of his ghostly servants build a small wooden dollhouse that fit perfectly into the nook in the far-right corner, with a matching nook meant for reading on the left. My bedroom hadn't changed since I was five, and it wasn't much, but I was going to miss it.

It was hard to believe that I was moving out on my own. I paused for a moment, letting out a deep breath as I listened to Shani talking nonstop in the background. Tomorrow marked the first day of the next chapter in my life. It was kind of crazy. Surreal even. And that was saying something since I was currently standing in an old bedroom in a castle behind the veil.

"Are you even listening to me?"

Shani's voice brought me back to the task at hand and I returned to putting things into boxes. "Yeah, I was just thinking about how insane it is that we are going to college. Tomorrow. I feel like we just graduated from junior high."

"I know!" Shani started talking a million miles a minute again and I walked back to my window to take one more look at my mystery guy before it got too late, and he went inside.

Pressing my forehead against the cold glass, I smiled seeing him run a hand through his dark hair and smiling a bit at the words he was reading. I then wondered what he was reading. What he was thinking.

I knew he couldn't see me out there in the blackness or through the veil, for that matter. It was not something a human could see. But then he looked up from his book and his brown eyes seemed to stare right back at mine. His brow furrowed, and he listed his head as if trying to make out something in the distance.

I lifted my hand in a sort of wave and I immediately felt like an idiot.

He can't see you, Calina.

His eyes continued to hold mine for another moment, and he slowly closed the book on his lap, still staring in my direction.

Could he see me?

"Oh my gosh, you're so obsessed!"

I jumped and looked back at Shani. "He's looking at me...it's like he can see..." I let my sentence die and waved her over to the window, but when I looked towards the cottage again, he had already gone inside.

She got up and stood next to me. "I don't see anything." She put her hand on my shoulder. "Let's go to bed. I'm exhausted and we have a big day tomorrow."

I nodded but didn't take my eyes off of the cottage still wondering if he had really seen me. He probably just saw an animal or something and it happened to be in this direction. No one could see through the veil without my dad's approval. Especially a human.

Right?

Chapter 2

St. Anne's Academy was located deep in the dark valley under a cover of a dense pine forest, far away from everything and hidden from Freyshire. Well, hidden from the humans there, anyway. The problem? It was located deep in the dark valley. Far away.

From everything.

Getting to the school was a feat in itself. I had been told how bad traffic sucked in the city, but nope. I could have guaranteed that it had nothing on forest traffic. When was the last time a human from Freyshire got stuck behind a pack of lazy hellhounds?

Exactly.

But once the forest thinned and I laid eyes on our destination, the annoying traffic suddenly seemed worth it. Plus, Shani was doing the driving since my dad wouldn't let me bring my car until after he had one of his ghastly servants rotate the tires.

I leaned my head out of the window of Shani's expensive little BMW letting my mouth hang open as we neared the enormous campus. It was as if we had driven into another world or traveled back to another time. Tall oak trees lined a mile-long drive up to the Academy, giving it one of the grandest entryways I had ever seen.

The main building towered above the rest, and it reminded me of a 15th century Tudor palace. Large brown bricks made up the foundation and it held an almost country-like charm with floor-to-ceiling windows and large verandas atop the two-story bump-outs along the entire front side of the building. The smaller buildings that dotted the rest of the campus were separated from the main house by vast gardens and stone paths.

I felt like I should have been dressed for a king's court and suddenly became overly self-conscious about my khaki shorts and tank top.

"Wow. This place is amazing!" Shani's half-sister, Reema, spoke up from the front seat. She swore that she had called 'shotgun' when we were packing up this morning, but I heard no such thing.

Reema pulled down the car vizor and flipped open the mirror. She dabbed at the sides of her glossed lips and fluffed her straight black hair. She was beautiful like Shani with the same thick jet-black hair and cocoa-colored eyes. But Reema's skin was a lighter shade of caramel than Shani's. I had always been jealous of their bronzed skin tones.

Watching Reema from the backseat, I thought about what my own make-up looked like. Or lack thereof. Shani said I didn't need it, but I still wore some. A little.

I leaned to the left and caught a glimpse of myself in the rearview. My porcelain skin looked even paler in the afternoon sun that came through the windows, and my dirty blonde hair made me appear even lighter. But I suppose I did have nice eyes. They were my mother's eyes. Hazel with little green specks in them.

Shani stuck her tongue out at me in the rearview mirror and we both laughed at each other's reflections. I hadn't even noticed that she had parked the car.

"You two are so immature. I can't believe we are actually the same age," Reema scoffed and rolled her eyes then gracefully exited the car as if she were stepping onto a red carpet. She even looked to both sides as if expecting paparazzi to rush her at any moment.

Shani and I both mocked Reema to each other's reflections and giggled again. Then Shani's expression turned serious. She nodded, probably more to herself than me. "Ok. Let's do this." She heaved a sigh then must have noticed me chewing on my nails in the rearview. "What's wrong?"

I took a break from my nervous nail biting and gulped. "What if coming to St. Anne's was a bad idea? I mean, was it such a bad thing to go to Freyshire College? We could have still had fun at a normal school."

Shani spun around in her seat to face me. "We talked about this. We aren't normal and going to Freyshire College would have just meant another four years in hiding. We can actually be ourselves at St. Anne's. You'll see. This new freedom to really get in touch with our...special talents is going to be amazing."

"I guess you're right."

"Of course I am." Shani grinned at me and patted my knee. "Now, come on. I don't want to be late."

▲ ▲ ▲ ▲

The three of us made our way along the paths that winded around the main building and through what appeared to be a fairy garden, then circled the student union to the auditorium. I was afraid we would get lost, but it was pretty hard to ignore the groups of water nymphs and purple Faeries all clutching large welcome packets who walked in front of us.

"I think we were supposed to check in somewhere. They all have packets and name tags." I pointed to a handsome Fae standing near the entrance of the auditorium. His long blond hair was pulled into a low ponytail that showed off his square jawline and pointed ears. I turned away when he made eye contact with those unbelievably bright baby-blues.

"I'm sure we can grab a packet on our way to the dorms," Shani said but was clearly making out with said Fae with her eyes. I watched in shock as he mouthed his number to her.

How did she do that? Not that I was completely shocked that guys and girls fell over themselves whenever they were in the presence of Shani. Her deep mocha skin was a perfect contrast to her thick black hair and espresso-colored eyes, and her smile was infectious. She was also on the petite side, making her that much more adorable.

A few of Shani's exes had confided in me that they think it was her demigod power that pulled them in initially, but I knew the truth. Shani was just about the most stunning person I had ever met. Inside and out. It was impossible not to be infatuated with her right off the bat.

Reema sighed and pushed us along. "Gross, Shani. I don't understand your taste at all."

Shani winked at the Fae cutie, and we fell into the line leading into the massive auditorium. It was decorated with the same medieval brick as the rest of the Academy's buildings, but inside near the stage, the walls were covered in thick velvet red and gold curtains. Intricate golden inlays spiraled up the mahogany pillars that stretched to the ceiling and met in the middle of, what appeared to be a hand-painted image of the Boleyn crest. A large shield-shaped item was in the center of the image, painted white with red bulls in its four corners.

"Ok, everyone, quiet down and take your seats." The tall woman in the middle of the auditorium stage cleared her throat and tapped on the microphone in front of her. "Yes, I think that'll work. Good morning, new students, and welcome to St. Anne's! Go Bulls!"

The crowd of students seated in the massive auditorium applauded and cheered. The woman on stage smiled wide, revealing two long fangs pointing out below her upper lip. I knew that there were vampires in the student body, but I was pleasantly surprised to find that there were some on the faculty too.

I was in definite need of their guidance.

Like most of the students at the Academy, I was a crossbreed. Basically, it meant that my parents were two different types of, well, creatures. And I was one of the unfortunate creatures who needed to learn how to control my bloodlust.

Dad was technically Fae, but my mom was a full vampire. It was kind of cool, I guess, because I did get some of the compulsion powers like controlling the minds of animals, and sometimes people.

Although I wasn't really good at using compulsion on people yet. Or animals. Honestly, I was kind of a lame vampire when it came to powers.

"I am Ms. Dunning, one of the Professors here at St. Anne's." She smiled again, retracting her fangs behind her full lips, and shook her long black hair off of her shoulder. The move was subtle but so incredibly graceful. She had to be full vamp. "I just wanted to welcome you all to orientation this morning and give you a run-down of what your day will look like. First, you will hear from our wonderful Headmaster, Dr. Rakesh Simon, then you will be going to your dormitories to meet your Resident Advisors and pick-up your course schedules. You will have about an hour in your dorms to relax, but then I want to have you all meet in front of the main house before noon.

"When you arrive in the front garden, you will locate the color-coded flag that corresponds with the color tab on your schedule. From there, you will take a tour of the campus with your smaller groups." Ms. Dunning let out a long sigh as if the itinerary had exasperated her. "Questions? No? Ok, let's welcome Headmaster Simon." She clapped her hands along with the students and exited the stage as the Headmaster made his way to the mic.

Headmaster Simon was intimidating. And that was putting it mildly. He had to have been at least 6'8", but his NBA player-like stature wasn't what made his presence so domineering. It was the two-inch canines that glittered beneath the fluorescent lights, and possibly the snout. Basically? He let his freak flag fly. He was a werewolf, and he didn't try to hide it by greeting us in his human form.

I shuddered as he padded up to the mic, his long claws screeching against the metal microphone stand. He stretched his black fur covered arms out wide, and before he spoke, his fangs retracted into his gums. His refined British accent was a stark contrast to his monstrous appearance. "Welcome, students. It is wonderful to have so many new, and 'special' faces here today. St. Anne's Academy has been home to creatures since 1536 when its namesake was executed for simply being herself." He paused as a booming outburst of applause filled the auditorium.

I cringed. The Academy was named after Anne Boleyn. And she was a vampire like me and many others sitting in the crowd. She was beheaded after people in the court discovered she was a creature, but instead of outing her, they thought it better that her death sentence be related to a story about her banging her brother. Honestly, I wasn't sure which offense was worse to be remembered for.

Dr. Simon waited for the roar of applause to quiet and continued with his welcome address. "Now, nearly 450 years later, we honor her sacrifice by offering a safe space for all creatures to learn and thrive as they enter adulthood. Our institution has been the stomping grounds for politicians, presidents, and world leaders, and, today, we are greeting the next generation of greatness."

A pang of nervous energy rushed through me. No, I was excited. It was an excited energy.

Right.

"I hope we have the same schedules this term." Shani whispered to my right while keeping her eyes on the Headmaster.

I turned and flashed her a brief smile, knowing full well we wouldn't have the same classes. She wanted to major in Economics, and I had a major case of the undecideds.

"All right, then. Welcome class of 2026! Go Bulls!" Headmaster Simon clapped loudly along with all of the students before sending us to our dorms.

The three of us stood and waited for the students in our row to make their way into the aisle. There must have been a few hundred people in our freshman class, all looking around excitedly and laughing with their friends that they came with and, probably, some they had just met.

I was just glad to have Shani. I had never been super outgoing like her and Reema. I honestly liked my time to myself.

"Stop trying to convince yourself that you like being a loner." Shani looped her arm through mine as we walked out of the auditorium. "This year is going to be all about trying new things and meeting new people. I'm going to help you come out of that shell of yours."

"I really hate when you read my mind like that. It's such an intrusion." I scowled at her, but I wasn't that angry. And she knew it.

She shrugged and gave me a wink, and we followed Reema down a covered walkway that led to the dormitories.

The dorms were laid out in several groups of four Tudor-style buildings, much like the main building, but connected together giving off an appearance of townhouses. We were assigned to the second building, called Reformation Hall. The school may have taken the Boleyn thing a bit too far, but it was kind of a cool name for a dorm.

And, of course, our room was located on the third floor. Thank the gods for movers.

Wandering down the tight hallway, I noticed that everyone's door had a whiteboard and markers on the wall beside it. The walls were lined with posters and flyers for different clubs and offers for tutors in just about every subject.

There were dozens of students moving from room to room, chatting and comparing schedules, and a large ogre nearly ran me over as he backed out into the hall from his room, trying to get a better angle on the giant couch he was moving.

I sighed in relief seeing the door to our room. It was all the way at the end of the hall across from the Resident Advisor's room.

Fantastic.

I was about to open our door when a short guy poked his head out of the Resident Advisor's room. "Hi there! You must be…" he paused and ran a bony finger down a list on a clipboard. "Reema, Shani, and Calina." He tapped the clipboard and looked up at us, a huge, and semi-creepy grin on his face. "I'm Chuck. I'm the RA on this floor. Welcome to Reformation Hall." He wiped his hand on his red and black St. Anne's sweatshirt then outstretched one of his bony arms. I crouched down slightly to shake his hand.

He was definitely a goblin.

We all shook hands and Chuck pulled a large bronze key from his tiny pant pocket. "Here, let me get the door for you. The locksmiths are still getting everyone's keys ready." He unlocked our room door then we all stood there a bit awkwardly, staring at each other.

"Right. Well, we are just going to pop into our room for a bit. We have a busy orientation schedule so…" I put my hand on the knob and waited for Chuck to go attend to someone else.

"Yes! Absolutely. Don't let me keep you. Just remember to pick up your keys by three o'clock this afternoon." Chuck smiled again and gave Reema a quick up and down before waddling down the hallway to the next newcomers.

"Ew." Reema looked like she just swallowed vomit.

"What? He's cute…I smell a first date! Literally." Shani laughed. She wasn't wrong, of course. Goblins did have a reputation for smelling a little less than fresh.

Reema stuck her pointed nose in the air. "Yuck. He looks like he's more your type anyway." She scoffed and pushed her way past Shani into the room.

"That was one time!" Shani called after her sister.

I reluctantly followed behind them, pausing in the small foyer and taking in the sight of my new home for the next four years. The dorm wasn't large, by any standards, but it wasn't tiny either. It was set up as more of a small apartment than a traditional dormitory. There was a kitchen to the right of the front door with white cabinets and black granite countertops, and a closet that contained the washer and dryer right across from it. The walls were painted in a soft grey and floor length bright white curtains hung from the large sliding glass door leading out to the balcony. The open concept boasted a shared living room and an eat-in dining nook that was already furnished with a comfy looking beige couch and a small wooden table. On either side of the living room wall, the dorm split off into two hallways, each with two rooms at the end.

Though the dorm room was meant for four students, we were the only three that would be staying there. Shani had begged her dad to make a call to ensure we wouldn't have to share our room with a stranger.

And Shani always got her way. Especially from Daddy-Set.

I made my way across the dorm and stepped out onto the balcony to a view of the entire campus. Leaning over the white metal railing, I watched as other students lugged suitcases and furniture into their own dorms. A minotaur was helping a strikingly beautiful Fae carry her large mirror up the steps, and a group of gorgons were tossing a football back and forth in the parking lot. There were so many different creatures wandering about and the entire scene was so surreal.

Growing up in Freyshire, I was used to keeping the creature side of me a well-kept secret; all of the creatures in town had to do the same. It was somewhat amusing since creatures could sense who around them shared a similar secret, and who was normal.

Meanwhile, our human counterparts had no idea that creatures were walking around, shopping at their stores, taking care of them as doctors or dentists, eating alongside them at restaurants, or going on dates with them. I had even dated several human boys all throughout high school, which was fun, but not being able to share all of myself with them was difficult. And a bit lonely.

But Shani was right. I could be myself here. There would be no judgment or hiding at St. Anne's.

I was about to call out to Shani and Reema to come and take in the view, but they were still arguing about their past boyfriends and one-night stands. I heaved a sigh and rested my forehead on the wall next to the balcony door. This was going to be a long semester.

Chapter 3

My first week at St. Anne's was a complete blur. Between getting lost in the five-story library and walking into the wrong class...twice..., I was beyond relieved that it was Friday.

Shani and I had plans to go into town to get dinner and drinks. And that was it. Seriously. I was *not* planning on going on a man hunt for my mystery guy. Besides, I had barely even thought about his perfectly symmetrical face. Or his stormy eyes. Or the way he semi-smiled while reading sometimes.

He hadn't crossed my mind. Not at all.

Plus, the population of Freyshire was pretty large, so the chances of randomly running into him somewhere in town were slim to none.

I would just have to wait until the next full moon to see him again.

"Whatcha doin'?" Shani plopped down beside me on a stone bench near the fountain in the back of the main house. It was my new favorite spot to just chill and people watch. I was still getting used to the fact that so many creatures were traipsing around in their supernatural forms without a care, and still continued to be amazed by it all.

"Nothing. Just relaxing before my next class. How was Alchemy?" I only asked that because I knew how much she was dreading taking the course. I was such a good friend.

"Ugh, you know I loathe that subject! It's a general-ed class, so I just have to suck it up and get through it. A 'C' is passing, right?"

I laughed, "Yes, 'C's get degrees'. And it's Friday, so at least we can go drink it off." I leaned my head on her shoulder. "Want to get Italian first?"

"Yeah, that sounds good." Shani nudged me slightly. "You know...you did make a deal with me last weekend."

I froze. Of course, she would remember that we talked about finding my mystery guy, but completely misremember the outcome. "I didn't forget our conversation, but you know I did not make any such deal."

"Whatever. I just don't see why we can't keep our eyes open. Where's the harm in that?"

I rolled my eyes and stood up. "Mmhmm, ok. I've got to get to class. See you in a bit."

It was my first day in Vampire Arts, and honestly, I was nervous. I was half vamp and all, but I was really bad at it.

When I entered the classroom, I was surprised to see an annex-looking room with a brick arch above five or six rows of two-person tables. The arched ceiling made the room appear that much longer and older. I found an empty table near the back of the room, but right in front of the floor-to-ceiling window.

Great. Not only could I embarrass myself in a class full of other vampires, but now I could potentially embarrass myself to anyone who happened to stroll by the building.

I lucked out in a way, because it wasn't a full class, and no one had to share a table with another student. At least there was that.

The Professor strode gracefully through the double doors and took her place at the front of the room. It was Ms. Dunning from the orientation. She was even more stunning close up.

"Good afternoon, students and welcome to Vampire Arts. You may recognize me from earlier in the week. I am Ms. Dunning and I have taught this class for almost a century now." She practically floated down the aisle between the tables as she personally greeted each of us.

When she approached my table, she held out her hand and I gave it a light shake. Her skin was cool and smooth like polished marble and her high cheekbones and bright, sapphire eyes gave her an elegant air.

I wanted to be her when I grew up.

I watched as she returned to the front of the room and introduced us to the content and expectations of the class. It was almost identical to the first-day announcements I had heard in all my other courses that week, and my mind began to wander.

I knew that I needed to pay attention because this class would be a struggle, but I couldn't help but think about that night.

What if we did run into...him? I mean, it was possible. Not probable, but...maybe. I swallowed hard, already scared to death at what I would say or do if I saw him out and about in real life. What if he thought I was a total weirdo? What if I totally fell on my ass right in front of him? What if—

"Miss Strovsky?"

I was immediately pulled out of my day-nightmare at the velvety rich voice coming from the front of the room. My eyes widened and I peered around at all the other students staring at me expectantly, some smirking at my apparent failure to pay attention.

Shit. What was I supposed to be saying? "I'm sorry, Ms. Dunning. Can you please repeat the question?"

She didn't seem pleased, and her mouth formed a tight line. "I was asking you all to share what powers you have as a vampire."

I sucked in a breath. "I can sometimes use compulsion on animals?" I wondered if Ms. Dunning could tell that I was lying.

"Sometimes?" Ms. Dunning was really staring me down.

I shrugged. She eyed me expecting more. So, I tried, "I've been practicing?" It came out as a question, and I wanted to crawl in a hole and die. I continued to hold in my breath as I avoided eye contact with everyone around me. I couldn't have been the only one, but it sure felt like I was the only vamp in the world that didn't have advanced powers.

"I see." After an eternity, she released me from her icy stare, and moved on to torture the next student.

I exhaled quietly, feeling sick to my stomach.

I really needed that drink with Shani.

▲▲▲▲

Luigi's Linguini was a cute little hole-in-the wall restaurant in the center of Freyshire. They had great food, and I loved the character of the place. As soon as you walked in you got smacked in the face with the strong scent of garlic and oregano.

No, I was not turned off by garlic. That was a common myth about vampires. I actually really loved garlic. Maybe not the smell of my breath after eating it, but that was what mints were for.

The inside of the restaurant matched the theme of the entire town. It was dark and medieval feeling with red brick on the interior walls and black iron sconces and chandeliers hung from corners and the ceiling. The owner preferred to use light bulbs rather than the candles that lined the main streets, but it still looked cool. And it was probably less of a fire hazard.

Shani and I grabbed a table in the corner of the restaurant, and I was not so pleasantly surprised to see Reema walk in and wave to us on her way to our table. Though I had a hard time stomaching hanging out with Shani's half-sister, I had to admit, she was a knock-out to look at. She moved through the rows of tables with ease, her slender hips swaying rhythmically like a well-timed dance as she walked. She was dressed in a tiny bright pink dress that could have easily been mistaken for underwear, but probably cost more than my entire wardrobe, and her straight black hair was slicked back into a low side bun. Her brilliantly white smile blinded me from the back of the restaurant as she beamed at us.

She was irritatingly perfect.

"I thought it was just going to be you and me tonight." I knew I was whining but hanging out with Reema meant listening to her talk about how great she looked and how many guys were checking her out.

"Sorry, she caught me as I was heading out the door," Shani said through a smile at her sister as Reema took an open seat.

"How did you two find this place? It looks kind of dumpy." Reema grimaced and picked her menu with two fingers as if it might give her a disease if she handled it for too long.

I gave Shani a kick under the table and frowned into my beer.

Reema leaned in closer to us, lowering her voice. "Anyway, did you guys see the elf that lives three rooms down the hall from us? Totally hot. I think I'm going to ask him out." She waved a server over with her perfectly manicured hand. "How was your first week? Any prospects?"

Reema was planning on majoring in Psychology, but in my opinion, she was really at the Academy to find her MRS degree. Since many of the graduates from St. Anne's went on to become politicians, or surgeons, or have other various wealthy and powerful careers, it made sense that Reema would want to scoop up a sugar daddy as soon as possible.

"Calina has one, don't you?" Shani elbowed me with a sly smile on her lips.

"Ooh, spill! Who is he?" Reema leaned in towards me.

"No one. I don't have any prospects." I elbowed Shani back.

"That's not true. We were actually going to search the town for him tonight."

I was seething. I hoped Shani would read my mind right now and shut up.

Reema clapped her hands together excitedly and, thankfully, our conversation was put on hold when the server came to take our orders.

I stared daggers at Shani, and she just stared back, smiling. As soon as the server left our table, Reema returned to her line of questioning about my potential relationship. I had to change the subject. Fast.

"Hey, you know who came by the dorm today?" I rested my elbows on the red checkerboard tablecloth and let my eyes shine with excitement.

Reema was intrigued and mirrored my expression. "Who?"

"Chuck." The corners of my mouth twitched, and I tried to keep a giggle in. "He was asking about you."

She tilted her head slightly and her brow furrowed, confused, and obviously not remembering who Chuck was.

"You remember Chuck. Our RA? He came by and said he saw you in his Chemistry lab. Thought he might ask you to study with him." I smiled wide and waited for Reema to picture our tiny goblin RA and get completely mortified.

"Chuck...Oh, gross!" Reema pursed her lips and sat back in her seat, crossing her arms over her chest. "As if I would ever talk to him, let alone study with him."

"Oh no." I inhaled sharp and bit my lip, feigning embarrassment. "I may have given him your number. I thought you might have been interested. Sorry...," I lied, now almost choking on the laugh that was busting through my lips.

Reema threw her napkin across the table at me. "You two are so immature."

"Hey, what did I do?" Shani was shocked at the accusation, but then she and I nearly rolled out of our chairs with laughter.

Reema searched the restaurant. "Where did our server go? I'm going to need a stronger drink."

▲▲▲▲

After listening to Reema complain about almost everything at Luigi's, the three of us strolled through downtown Freyshire. There was something about the little town that was thrilling and magical. It was always a little bit dark and mysterious, and the buildings were ancient with thousands of years of secrets that were hidden in their walls and whispered throughout the narrow alleyways. And with the added component of creatures hiding in plain sight among the townspeople, Freyshire was that much more mystical.

Our heels click-clacked over the cobblestone street and we walked arm in arm on our way to the part of town famous for its nightlife. There was already a line of people outside of Bloody Goode's, a tiny little bar that had the best beer selection, and surprisingly, amazing martinis and held an open mic night every Friday.

We paid our entry fee and wandered through a long and narrow hallway that opened up into a crowded room that resembled someone's basement. The walls were painted black and plastered with concert posters and photos of the owners with various celebrities. The smell of stale beer and cigarettes invaded my nostrils, but even with the overwhelming dinginess, it was still one of my favorite hangouts.

I was able to snag us a table near the stage that was on the opposite side of the room while Shani and Reema went to the bar to grab us some blood-orange martinis.

Yes, I was aware that the bar's name had the word, "blood" in it and was famous for their *blood* orange martinis, and that I was, technically, a vampire. But it was really just a coincidence. A comical coincidence. There was no blood in the drinks and the owner, Mr. Goode, was a human that must have found the play on words amusing.

"One martini." Shani placed the bright red drink in front of me and she and Reema sat down to listen to a tall girl finish up her set on stage. She took a bow, and the crowd gave her a hardy round of applause.

When she stepped off the stage and we were waiting for the next act, I lifted my drink and faced my friends. Well, my friend and her half-sister. "To our first year of college."

"To our first boyfriends. Or maybe just one-nighters." Reema winked and she and I clinked our glasses together, a few drops splashing over the rims. I held my glass mid-air waiting for Shani to take part in our celebration, but she was focused on the stage, her eyes wide and her grin even wider.

Curious, I turned to the stage and almost dropped my drink onto the table. A young and handsome guy was taking his place on the lone stool in front of the microphone, acoustic guitar in hand. I stared for a solid minute then realized my mouth was hanging open like a puppy with its head out the car window.

"Well, hello, handsome."

Reema's voice pulled me back into reality. But I couldn't stop staring. His brown eyes and symmetrical features angled shyly toward his hands as he geared up for his set. He gave a semi-smile to the crowd. The same semi-smile he had when he read his books. Not that I remembered it, really.

"Oh my gods, Cali. It's him." Shani squealed and leaned over the table towards me, her excitement threatening to explode out of her.

"Wait, 'him'? Like, the same 'no one' we were talking about at dinner?" Reema eyed me suspiciously, then turned her gaze to my mystery man. "Wow. You have nice taste."

I could see the wheels turning in her head but didn't really think much of it. I was too distracted by the fact that the guy I had been stalking...no, noticing...was here. *Here.* He was real. Tangible. And twenty feet away from me.

He smiled again, and sheepishly looked down at his strings. "Ok, this is new so...so, be kind." His fingers began to pick at the strings, gently at first, then he picked up speed, but still in full control of his instrument.

I watched him intently, holding my breath waiting for him to start singing.

His voice was like velvet, smooth and beautiful, and it layered the bar with a soft and contented feeling that I couldn't explain.

No one moved. Or spoke. He drew in the attention of the crowd with ease and when he finished, he gave a sort of head nod as a bow that brought us all to our feet. He stood from the stool and put a hand through his thick hair, smiling.

I was clapping so hard that my palms stung. Shani was bouncing up and down on her toes, and even Reema was applauding. Kind of.

He moved to the stage steps and paused as he met my eye. His brow furrowed slightly, and he focused on me for a moment, as if he recognized me. I held his gaze, and my body went rigid with nerves, my heart about to thud right out of my chest.

Suddenly uncomfortable under the weight of his stare, I focused on my unfinished martini. When I finally found the courage to stop eyeing the liquid in my glass, I looked back up at the stage and he was gone.

Reema sipped her drink. "That was incredible."

My heart was still beating uncontrollably, and I was a bit breathless.

Incredible Indeed.

Chapter 4

I couldn't concentrate.

It had been three weeks since going to open mic night at Bloody Goode's and I had literally thought of nothing else. I would have been lying if I said that I didn't "accidentally" show up to open mic night the last two Friday's hoping to see him, but he hadn't been there. I would have also been lying if I said that I wasn't overly excited to spend this weekend at my dad's for the full moon.

"Cali, just ask the manager who was on the set list the night we were there." Shani's voice had an edge to it, and she slammed a book shut on her desk.

"What?"

"You've been obsessing over this guy for weeks. Just ask the manager at the bar who he is. They have to have a list or something."

"Why do I have to continuously ask you not to invade my thoughts?" I leaned my hip against my dresser with my arms crossed.

"It's really hard to ignore your thoughts when they are so incredibly needy and laced with desperation." She placed her head in her hands and seemed frustrated. "I'm sorry," she said into her palms.

I forgot my annoyance for the moment. "What's wrong?" I went over to her bed and sat down so I could face her.

"It's this stupid class. My mid-term is next week, and I am totally going to fail. I even tried getting a tutor, but I haven't found anyone yet."

"Isn't Reema looking for someone to help her in Chemistry? Maybe you could share if she finds a tutor. They might be good at Alchemy...it's basically the same thing, right?"

She let her forehead hit the desk. "Between this and my Mythology class, I am screwed. My dad is going to kill me."

"How are you failing Mythology? Isn't that, like, family history for you?"

Shani looked at me wearily, then we both started to laugh. "Look, I'm sorry for snapping at you. I don't actually think you're needy, but damn, Cali, go find out who this guy is so we can all move on."

"I am going to dad's this weekend, so at least I'll see him again."

Shani just shook her head at me. "Oh, you poor pitiful girl."

I was about to protest her unsaid accusation of me being unwilling to make the first move when my phone rang on my desk. I narrowed my eyes at Shani. "We will continue this later."

She simply frowned and went back to her textbook.

"Hey, mom," I said into the receiver as I answered the call. My mother's heavy Polish accent came through on the other end.

"Calina, it's been so long since you've called your mother!" She sounded distracted and I pictured her sitting on her king-sized bed filing her long nails while getting a foot massage from her man candy of the week.

I sighed. "Mom, I just talked to you yesterday." I glanced over to Shani who was now laughing to herself while unintentionally eavesdropping.

"Well, that was yesterday. Who knows what could have happened in the last twelve hours." Her voice grew muffled, and I could hear rustling. "No...to the left..."

"Mom."

"Sorry, darling. When are you coming by the house? I can make you your favorite meal. I'm sure you're tired of the same old student cafeteria food. I could even throw some B+ into the cheese mix if you want." She almost sounded as if she were begging, and I was surprised at her uncharacteristic tone.

I had to admit that the dinner invitation sounded amazing. B+ was hard to come by as far as blood goes. As a half-vampire, I craved blood on a daily basis, but I was also lucky enough to be able to survive on normal food. And my favorite meal was my mom's homemade perogies. The recipe was my great-grandmothers from the early 1400's and it was to die for. In fact, I'm pretty sure someone had.

"I can't come this weekend, mom. I'm going to dad's for the full moon."

My mother was silent on the other end of the line, and I could practically hear her teeth grinding in frustration. "I see. Well, you were always a daddy's girl. I suppose I can wait another weekend since you would rather spend your time with that...thing."

Now it was my turn to be frustrated. "That 'thing' is my dad. And I only see him once a month. I promise I will come over and see you on Monday." I waited for her to acknowledge my offer. "Mom?"

She sighed dramatically. "Fine. Until Monday." With that she hung up the phone and I stared blankly at the 'Call Ended' screen. She was just so...

"Needy."

I looked up at Shani as she responded to my exact thought. I just shook my head, annoyed but not surprised by my mother's behavior.

Shani held up her Mythology textbook. "Parents. Am I right?"

I nodded. "On that note, it's time to go and see the other one."

▲ ▲ ▲ ▲

I saw my dad only once a month on the full moon, but nevertheless, we were actually pretty close. He always asked me about school and my friends and made sure to cover all of the necessary "parent" topics like sex, drugs, and rock and roll. He had always seemed a little uncomfortable during some of the talks, but he still made the effort. I think he felt guilty about not being able to be around too much when I was growing up.

He and my mom split soon after I was born, which wasn't a shocker being that he was the king of the other side and all. Plus, my mom could be a little extra sometimes. She was spontaneous and overdramatic, and she never wanted to settle down, but tried her best to be a good mom. And she was. Except on days when the bloodlust would hit her. Then I wouldn't see her for days, sometimes weeks, at a time.

I was not looking forward to that part of my vampirism. And apparently, it was supposed to get more intense and more frequent as I got older. As if being a woman dealing with hormonal changes wasn't hard enough already.

But, truthfully, having divorced parents wasn't the worst. I got two Christmases and during full moons, I could come hang out with dad behind the veil where the parties were on point. Especially during the Wild Hunt.

"So, how are you doing in your courses this semester?" My dad appeared genuinely interested in my time at the Academy as he bit into a massive turkey leg. His icy-blue eyes demanded my attention and stood out against the near translucent paleness of his skin.

They were both my most and least favorite qualities of his. Beautiful and haunting, and especially terrifying when I was in trouble.

"Good. I'm making A's. Well, in all of my classes but Vampire Arts." I quickly took a bite of boiled potatoes so I wouldn't have to go into more detail.

He lowered his fork and glanced up at me from his dinner plate, a stern look on his face. "Calina—"

"Forgive my intrusion, my Lord, but you are needed in the stables." A transparent farm hand floated near the doorway.

Phew, saved by the ghost.

My dad stood. "We will continue this conversation upon my return."

"Can't wait," I said with a huff.

He stopped and gave me the look that always made me cower when I was a kid. He was a sweet man, but geez he could be scary sometimes.

"Sorry."

He shook his head with the classic disappointed dad face and walked out, leaving me alone with my thoughts and uneaten dinner. I swirled the tines of my fork through the vegetables and potatoes on my plate allowing my mind and eyes to wander around the drafty and enormous dining room.

I had been to my dad's place thousands of times but was always stunned by the elegance of the old castle. Even though it was ancient and layered in centuries of dust, the gray columns that flanked each floor-to-ceiling window made the halls look so grand. Candle-lit chandeliers lined the great hall and lush crimson and silver Turkish rugs covered the cold marble floors. Large paintings that depicted different parts of the grounds and family members who had long since been dead crowded the foyer and the staircase that wound up and around the walls to the second story.

It was dark and a little damp feeling, but with a little bit of elbow grease, the place could have really been something.

"His Grace has instructed me to tell you he will be gone for the evening and that you should finish dinner and tend to your studies." The raspy voice of one of my dad's huntsman/servants interrupted my thoughts of contacting someone from HGTV to assist me with a home makeover.

"Thank you." I smiled politely at the messenger. Figures. Well. I supposed I avoided another father-daughter conversation about how I needed to apply myself more in school.

I put down my fork, not hungry anyway, and retreated to my room. It was almost seven o'clock, and I settled down on my bed to do my homework, but it was nearly impossible to get a single thought written.

The only thing on my mind was when *he* would be going outside to read. I had looked forward to my weekend at dad's ever since I heard him play at Bloody Goode's.

Wow, my behavior *was* really becoming creepy.

I turned on the TV to distract myself. I would not go to the window. Would not check to see if he is out there. Would not watch him. Nope. I flipped through the hundreds of crappy channels at least three times then turned off the tube. Rolling onto my back, I reached for my pillow and covered my face with it.

This was ridiculous.

I jumped off my bed and skipped over to the window. Just like every other night I had been there, there he was. Sitting in his white chair, book in hand. And now that I had seen him play, heard him sing, he was that much more attractive. And even more of an enigma.

I watched him for a couple more minutes, daydreaming of when I might be able to speak to him. In person. And not just think about talking to him from the safety of my dad's house behind the veil.

Then he caught me by surprise. He was looking at me. *Really* looking. It was like he was actually seeing *me* this time, and not just some animal in the dark distance.

I dared to lift my hand in a wave, just as I had last month, not expecting a reaction.

And then it happened. He stood, keeping his brown eyes locked with mine, and waved back.

Chapter 5

"You're joking."

"No, I swear. He waved at me. He was seeing me. Through the veil!"

Shani eyed me suspiciously, chewing on her lower lip as if she were deciding if I was lying to her or not. "It's impossible. Humans can't even see the veil, and especially not behind it. Hell, I'm not sure that most creatures can see behind the veil."

"I know. But it happened."

She jumped up from the bench we had been meeting at in between classes, suddenly grinning. "This is great news. It means something. I can feel it." She bounced on her toes and shook my shoulders excitedly. "You've got to talk to him. This Friday. We can go back to Bloody Goode's."

"Whoa, I don't think we need to break the boundaries of the stalker-stalkee relationship just yet. It was probably just my imagination or something. Besides, we can't guarantee that he will even be playing Friday." I prayed she would agree with me. My stomach was already twisting into knots at the mere thought of speaking to him. I'd probably be puking on his shoes if I were actually speaking to him.

Shani still smiled at me, and I knew she was reading my thoughts. Again. I was about to shame her for it, but then a fantastic idea came to me. I met her gaze and my eyes widened. Her brow furrowed slightly then she started shaking her head.

"No, absolutely not."

"Come on, Shani, please? It's just once. I just want to know if he recognizes me. Before I try to strike up a conversation."

She crossed her bronzed arms over her chest and avoided eye contact.

"Please. For me. Besides, you never seem to have a problem reading *my* thoughts."

She frowned. "That's not fair. You're my best friend. He's a stranger...it would be a violation..."

"And it's not a violation when you do it to me?"

She pursed her lips and appeared to be contemplating the idea.

I gave her my best puppy-dog face and considered trying out my compulsion power on her. Not that it would work on a demigod. "Please. I have to know. I need to know that I'm not crazy."

Her lips slowly curved upward. "Well, you *are* crazy. But I guess I can help just this once."

I leaped up and threw my arms around her. "Thank you!"

She didn't hug me back. "You owe me."

△ △ △ △

Friday came quickly. Too quickly.

I was nauseous all week, thinking of what I was going to say to him if we managed to see him tonight. He hadn't been back to an open mic night in over a month, so I am not sure why my nerves were hitting me so hard. I probably wouldn't see him anyway.

Shani helped me get ready for my "big night". At least, that's what she had been referring to it as all week long. She pulled my long hair into a messy bun that allowed a few strands to fall and frame my cheekbones. I even let her put a touch of make-up on me. I stared at my reflection in the floor-length mirror while I waited for Shani to finish doing her own hair. The dress that I had borrowed from Reema gently hugged my very small curves and hung just below my knees. I was a bit nervous about the spaghetti straps showing too much of my pale skin, but the deep green hue of the fabric was perfect and brought out my eyes.

Shani came and stood next to me. Beautiful and perfect as always in her bright yellow off-the-shoulder top and tight jeans. She leaned her shoulder on mine. "You look gorgeous. Even if he didn't really see you behind the veil, he will definitely notice you tonight."

"Thanks. Is Reema coming?" Please no.

"No, she said she is studying tonight. More like going to get her Botox shot tonight." Shani and I busted out laughing and headed out of our dorm.

We walked down the dark cobblestone streets toward Bloody Goode's. I expected there to be a long line out front, but instead, the owner had opened up the outside patio. Tables were set up along the side of the building with small fairy lights draped from the roof to the ends of the poles on each corner of the patio. There was a romantic small-town feel to the set up that felt so foreign when compared to the dank and dirty inside of the bar.

I smiled when I noticed the corner of the patio set up with speakers and a stool. I pointed to a table. "Shall we?" Shani and I took our seats, and a server swiftly took our drink orders. The server took a quick interest in Shani, twirling her hair and blushing every time Shani flashed her brilliant smile in the server's direction. Her name tag said "Sarah" and she might have been twenty or twenty-one, and insanely cute with a shoulder length blonde bob and a smear of freckles that dotted her petite nose.

And Sarah was definitely a creature. That was something that most non-humans could detect pretty easily. Although, it was nearly impossible to guess what kind of creature someone was. Sarah gave Shani a tiny wink before running off to collect our drinks from the bar.

Shani's grin was plastered on her face as she watched her new romantic interest rush away. I nudged her shoulder. "She's cute."

"Hmm? Oh. I hadn't noticed." Shani giggled and wrote her number down on the bar napkin, carefully folding it and ready to exchange it with our drinks when Sarah returned. Sarah happily took the napkin and beamed as she placed our drinks on the table.

I swirled my straw in my drink after our server placed them in front of us. I was happy for the distraction of watching Shani and Sarah flirt with each other. It kept me from focusing on the nervous mess that I was in that moment. I swallowed hard, a wave of nausea roiling through my stomach. What if he was actually here? What if I actually had to talk to him? What if—

"Stop. It's going to be fine."

I looked at Shani and nodded, but I didn't believe her. Suddenly the patio erupted in applause, and I turned my chair to face the make-shift stage.

It was him.

I kicked Shani's foot under the table, and she nodded but didn't look at me. She was trying to read his thoughts. I couldn't imagine how hard it must be to do that with all the noise and distractions. But I guess she was Set's daughter, so she was used to focusing during complete chaos. And creating it.

I held my breath. Waiting. Daydreaming. He walked to the stool and the owner tapped on the mic.

"It's Friday night, and that means Open Mic! Let's welcome to the stage, Oliver Chase." The owner clapped his hands and took his exit, leaving Oliver to his audience.

Oliver.

It was a perfect name for him. He fumbled with his guitar as he sat on the stool and adjusted the microphone. Then, when he glanced up to talk to the crowd, his brown eyes landed on me. He squinted in recognition, ever so slightly, then his fingers strummed the strings, and he looked down at his hands.

I exhaled, feeling the burning in my chest from holding my breath so long and swallowed down the bile that was creeping up my throat, adding physical pain to my mental anguish.

"He's seen you before. But he thinks he imagined it. He's...confused." Shani stared at Oliver singing on stage for another second then sat back in her chair. She picked up her martini and took a long sip. "He thinks you're beautiful. He also thinks you'd look even better without your clothes on." She smiled at me, seemingly proud of her supernatural abilities.

"Ok, leave some for the imagination." I threw an olive at her as heat flushed my neck and cheeks.

"Hey, I can't help it that guys think about sex so much!" She laughed and tossed the unwanted fruit back at me.

I watched Oliver while simultaneously wringing my hands, but as his voice rang through the outside oasis, my nerves lessened. It was just like the first time I heard him play. The soft melody of his voice and strumming blanketed the air with a cool ease. I closed my eyes, allowing my thoughts to settle, getting lost in the sound.

I'd never heard anything like it. Or felt anything like it. It was...magical.

"Excuse me."

I jolted from my reverie, knocking over my drink. I was horrified to see it dripping from the table and from his shirt.

Oliver's shirt. I hadn't even realized his song had ended.

I gulped. "I-I'm so sorry." I panicked and grabbed a drink napkin, dabbing it gently on Oliver's gray hoodie. "I'm so so sorry."

I realized what I was doing and stopped abruptly, now meeting his eye. Shani just stared in absolute horror.

Oliver smiled and gently took the napkin from my trembling hand. "It's my fault. I didn't mean to scare you. I, uh...this is going to sound crazy, but I think I know you." Now it was Oliver who was absently dabbing his shirt with the already soaked napkin. His lips made a thin line, and he looked like he was grappling with something. "I mean...have we met?"

He stopped wiping his hoodie and put the napkin down on the table as if he realized that he was fidgeting. His eyebrow raised and he looked expectantly at me.

I opened my mouth to say something but couldn't formulate a sentence. Dammit, he was cute.

"I'm Shani. And this is Calina." Shani reached her arm over the table and held her hand out to shake Oliver's. "Want to join us?" She motioned to the empty chair adjacent to mine, but Oliver didn't seem to hear her invitation and stood there, his eyes still fixated on mine.

Suddenly, I discovered that I could, in fact, speak. I cleared my throat. "Yes, hi. I'm Cali." He shook both our hands and the warmth lingered in my palm when he pulled his hand away. "I don't think we've met. I've seen you though." Shani kicked me, her eyes widening but staying on Oliver.

Her smile appeared to be plastered on her face. "We saw you play a few weeks ago."

"Right, I saw you play. Here." I silently thanked the gods that Shani had rescued me.

"Oh. That must be it. I'm Oliver." He stood there awkwardly for a moment then finally took a seat at our table. "Sorry, I didn't want to interrupt..."

"Please, you aren't interrupting. We were just saying how good your song was, right, Cali?"

His eyes were even more soulful up close. Well, from not behind my window. I could definitely get lost in there.

"Cali?" Shani laughed nervously, nudging my elbow with hers. "Oliver's really good. Right?"

"What? Um, yes, you were really great up there. How long have you been playing?" I could hear the shaking of my voice, but I needed him to carry this conversation as I obviously couldn't function.

"Thank you. I've played since I was five. But honestly, I've only come to an open mic night two other times. I've got horrible stage fright." His easy smile made me more uneasy.

"You'd never be able to tell. You sounded like you've been performing forever." Thank goodness for Shani being able to talk to anyone. What the hell was wrong with me?

"I appreciate that." Oliver's gaze casually landed on me again and we held each other's eyes just a moment too long. He looked away and cleared his throat. "I guess I should probably get going. Thank you for talking with me for a bit." He stood slowly as if waiting for one of us to say something to make him stay.

I still couldn't get my mouth to say any of the things that were going through my mind. *You're the most beautiful boy*

I've ever seen. Your voice is like a velvet blanket that I want to have wrapped all around me for the rest of my life. I think we would make gorgeous musical vampire babies together.

You know. Normal things someone would say to a guy they just met.

The only thing I could manage was a smile as he locked eyes with me once more. He turned as if he was about to walk away, then stopped and spun on his heel back toward our table.

"Do you maybe want to go get dessert? There's a café down the road. They have amazing cheesecake." He shook his head, looking down at the ground. He rubbed the back of his neck which was turning more crimson by the second. "That sounded less lame in my head."

His eyes still held mine captive. His gaze piercing and deep. I couldn't take it. "We actually have to get—"

"We'd love to." Shani spoke over me then stood, motioning for me to follow.

I was going to kill her.

Chapter 6

We followed Oliver from the safety and familiarity of the bar down a darkened alley. This was a bad idea. That was how horror movies started. I mean, we didn't know this guy. He could have been a serial killer, for gods' sake.

"Relax. There are scarier things walking right next to me." Shani looped her arm through mine.

Right. I supposed I could have protected us if needed. I mean, I was half vamp after all.

Oliver stopped walking when we approached a tiny hole-in-the-wall café at the end of the alley. I'd never been there, or even known that it existed. The café took up the corner spot in an old building and its windows faced the street on either side. I could see several red booths and a white counter with stools lined alongside it.

It was totally retro. And completely different from all of the other places in Freyshire. How had I never heard of this place?

Oliver pulled open the glass door, '*Mama's Place*' printed in white lettering on the pane, then held it open for us to walk in before him.

Ok, one point for Oliver. I loved a guy with basic manners.

"This place is kind of old and it doesn't look like much, but the lady who owns it bakes everything herself." Oliver flashed a half smile, thrusting his hands into his pant pockets. He rocked back and forth on his heels before leading Shani and I to a booth next to the window.

Was it possible that Oliver was even more nervous than I was?

"Oh shoot." Shani stopped in front of the booth and spun on her heel to face me. "I totally forgot. I have to pick Reema up. From her study group thing. Remember?"

I stared at her in shock. I was *really* going to kill her.

She gave me a wink, then looked at Oliver. "You guys have fun. It was so nice to meet you. Ok, byeee!"

"Shani—," I tried.

She wiggled her fingers in a wave and quickly raced out of the café. Oliver still had his hands stuffed into his pockets and shrugged.

"Do you need to go with her?"

Come on, Cali, you can do this. I managed a smile through a new onset of nausea. "No, it's ok. Let's get some cheesecake."

Oliver sat across the booth from me and grabbed one of the laminated menus from behind the salt and pepper shakers. He acted as if he was perusing multiple options of cheesecakes then clumsily placed the menu back where he got it.

"We could have regular cheesecake or regular cheesecake. With strawberry sauce."

"Hmm, so many choices." I pretended to ponder my decision. "How about the regular cheesecake?"

"Bold choice."

An old woman hobbled over to our booth to take our order and Oliver appeared relieved as he ordered two slices of the dessert. The woman nodded and walked back behind the counter.

Oliver watched her leave and drummed his fingers on the table then stared at me point blank. "I'm nervous. Is it obvious?"

I let a giggle escape. "Only slightly." I briefly wondered if I should share the fact that I was literally battling away the vomit that was sure to explode out of my mouth if I said too much.

"A laugh. That's good. I'm sorry, I feel like I'm all over the place. It's just, when I saw you tonight from the stage, I couldn't shake the feeling that I'd seen you before. And not from another open mic night."

I wanted to tell him about the veil. Tell him that we had seen each other, and it hadn't been his imagination. But that would mean telling him about, well, everything. And I didn't think that was a good conversation to have on the first date. If it was a date. Which it wasn't.

"Maybe I just have one of those faces."

"No, I've never seen anyone that looks quite like you." His breath caught as if he wanted to say more, but instead he scratched at an invisible speck of dirt on the table.

I chewed on the inside of my cheek, praying my pale skin wasn't beet red. "So. Do you go to Freyshire College?"

He seemed happy for a change of subject. "Yeah, it's my first year. You?"

"I go to a...um...private university. It's really small. What are you majoring in?"

"Honestly? I haven't chosen one yet." Oliver's shoulders seemed more relaxed as he spoke. "I got a scholarship to play lacrosse and my mom really wants me to go into Medicine...but..." He shrugged.

"But you don't want to be a Doctor."

"Not even a little. Blood makes me a little squeamish."

That was not something we had in common.

His brown eyes sparkled under the fluorescent lights hanging over the booth. "I'm not convinced that choosing a career path at nineteen is a great idea. How do you even know who you are at nineteen?"

"Sounds like something that someone with absolutely no clue about what they want to do would say."

"Ah. Ok, I see how it is." A mischievous smile played on his lips. "Then, what is it that you have chosen to focus on as your life's ambition?"

I tried hard to keep a straight face. "I'm not convinced that choosing a career path at nineteen is a great idea."

Oliver laughed, a perfect sound that rang through my ears. It was impossible not to notice the dimple that formed just above the left side of his lips when he smiled so big.

I laughed too, my nervousness fading.

The server came back with our cheesecakes and set the plates in the middle of the table, along with two forks.

Oliver held up his fork and tilted it to me. "To having no clue."

I lifted my fork and tapped it to his in a toast. "To having no clue."

▲▲▲▲

Oliver and I decided to take a walk after eating the most amazing cheesecake I had ever tasted.

Seriously, how had I never heard of *Mama's*?

It was a humid evening which made the cobblestone streets gleam underneath the candlelit streetlamps, dew glistening as if it had just finished raining. I loved walking through Freyshire at night. And walking with Oliver as he talked on and on about his favorite books and songwriters right next to me made it that much more enchanting.

He walked so close to me that our shoulders brushed every couple of steps and simultaneously sent warmth and shivers all along my spine. I wanted nothing more than to wrap my arm around his and intertwine my fingers with his.

The feeling was absolute torture, yet I didn't want our walk to end.

"You're pretty quiet. I hope I'm not talking your ear off." Oliver slowed his pace slightly as we approached a street vendor selling coffee. "Is it too late for a coffee?"

"It's never too late for coffee."

My entire being flushed hot when he grasped my hand in his and pulled me across the street to the vendor. When we got up to the counter, he must have realized that he was still holding my hand and awkwardly pulled his away, thrusting it through his wavy brown hair.

Gods, he was adorable.

We sipped our coffees in comfortable silence as we continued our stroll through the damp streets.

"So, tell me about you. How long have you lived in Freyshire?" Oliver just had to go and break the silence.

My heartbeat quickened. I needed to be careful of how I worded things about my family. And me. "Most of my life. My mom was an immigrant and I think this town reminds her of home." Mostly due to the fact that she was born in 1702 and Freyshire hadn't undergone many changes in the form of progress since around that time.

"And your dad?" Oliver studied my profile as we walked, truly interested in what I had to say. It was refreshing. Most of the guys I had dated in the past could have cared less about me or my interests.

"My parents got divorced right after I was born. Different temperaments." I smiled to myself thinking about how they can't be in the same room without arguing. "My mom got custody of me, but my dad and I are still close though. I only see him once a month since he lives...so far away."

"That's nice that you two are still close. My dad passed when I was a toddler, so I don't really remember much about him. It has always just been me and my mom and two older sisters." He looked off into the distance, and for the briefest moment, a hint of sadness was in his eyes. He covered it up as quickly as it had appeared as he chuckled, "There's a lot of estrogen in my house. But it's probably a good thing."

"You're lucky. I don't have any siblings. Shani is the closest thing I have to a sister, and she is about all I can handle."

We both laughed a little then continued on. Oliver's arm brushed against mine again then the back of his hand rested on mine just before he laced his fingers around mine. I could hear the quickening of his pulse and the sound of his heart beating wildly in his chest.

My breath caught in my throat, and I closed my fingers around his.

"You never did tell me where you go to school."

Shit.

"Oh, you probably wouldn't know it...St. Anne's?" I prayed he wouldn't ask me about it and took a long drink to avoid saying more.

"St. Anne's? Is that..." He trailed off, seemingly trying to recall if he'd ever heard about it.

Double shit.

"Oh, you mean the Catholic academy in the valley." It was more of a statement than a question and he nodded to himself before I confirmed. "I think my school's lacrosse team plays against St. Anne's this season."

"Yep. That's the one." Yikes, that was close. Not that St. Anne's was a secret. It was just that the entire student body wasn't exactly human. And too many questions led to too many lies, which led to way too much to keep track of. In fact, St. Anne's Academy had a decent reputation for putting out many of the world's leaders and CEOs. Turned out that creatures were pretty darn intelligent. Or just really good at human control and manipulation.

Tomato, Ta-mah-to.

"I think I've heard that it's a pretty good school." He emptied his cup and tossed it in a nearby garbage can. He seemed to be stalling somehow. His nervous energy had returned and was almost palpable.

He turned to face me. "Calina, I..." He searched my face, his eyes moving from mine to my lips and back. His hand still gripped mine as he looked at me. A cool breeze moved around us, and a shudder ran throughout my body. He leaned a little closer toward me and his other hand reached up as if he were about to brush a strand of hair from my face, but he let it fall back to his side.

From out of nowhere, the breeze grew into forceful wind gusts, swirling around us, encircling us in that moment. I felt a rush of enchantment and romanticism with the billowing winds. I held my breath. He was going to kiss me. I wanted him to kiss me. My lips parted slightly, and I inched forward.

Oliver did not seem to agree with me on the romantic weather and suddenly backed away slightly while peering anxiously around as the winds continued to pick up. He studied my face a moment, his expression unreadable, then turned away again. The gusts of wind came to an abrupt halt, and he gently removed his hand from mine. "Can I walk you back to your car?"

What? I was momentarily glued to my spot, completely thrown. I stood a little straighter and had to basically unpucker my lips. "Um, yeah. Thanks."

Chapter 7

To say that I had been obsessing over the moment of my near kiss with Oliver was an understatement. I was in a state of complete shock. And panic. What did I do wrong? Was it something I said?

"You did nothing wrong. He was probably just nervous and didn't want to rush anything." Shani and I sat on our bench in the middle of the campus creature watching. We'd been sitting in the same spot for over an hour after our classes let out and had already seen two elves, six vampires, and a swarm of fairies...it was an incredibly diverse college campus.

"It was so weird though, Shani. You should have seen how he looked at me. It was like he wanted me to do or say something, and I couldn't live up to his expectations."

She shook her head. "I think you're overthinking the situation. Has he texted you? Called?"

I raised an eyebrow.

"Right, no one calls people anymore. I would see if he texts you today. There is no way that he won't. His thoughts when he saw you were...let's just say I felt uncomfortable." Shani blushed and laughed to herself.

I nodded. Hopefully she was right, and he was just nervous.

"Hey, nerds." Reema gave us her overly sweet smile that dripped with fakeness as she strode over to the bench. "Can I join you?" She didn't wait for a response and sat down almost on top of me, and I scooted over to make some room and avoid being squashed.

"So, I hear you had an impromptu date last night." Reema examined her nails, pursing her lips. "How was it?"

I seethed and gave a sideways glance to Shani, hoping she knew how irritated I was that she told Reema about my outing. Shani didn't look back at me, but I could have sworn she was fighting a smile.

"It wasn't a date. We just went to get some dessert and coffee after his show."

"Mmhmm. And?"

"And what?"

"How was the kiss?" Reema narrowed her eyes at me. "Sex?"

I gaped at her.

"What? He's hot. Sex would definitely have been on my mind after dessert and coffee."

I rolled my eyes. "Well, I'm not as...forward—"

"Experienced," she interrupted. "You're not as experienced."

I let out a slow exhale trying to control the anger taking over. "Sure. Whatever. We didn't have sex. We didn't even kiss."

"Pity." Reema shrugged. "Guess I can let you know how good a kisser he is after tonight."

Now Shani decided to join the conversation. "What are you talking about?"

"Oliver. Oh no, I completely forgot to tell you that I found a tutor. Turns out Oliver's really good at Chemistry. He must have found my request on TutorHelp.com."

"How do you know it's even the same guy we're talking about?"

"He called me yesterday to ask about my tutoring post. Must have been before your little date. Anyway, we got to talking and he was telling me all about his singing...I put two and two together." Reema stood excitedly and blew us each a kiss. "See you girls later. Hopefully not until tomorrow, if all goes well tonight." She crossed her fingers and winked at me before waltzing away.

Bitch.

"I'm so sorry, Cali, I had no idea Oliver was her new tutor." Shani put her hand on my shoulder.

I shrugged. Maybe that's why he hadn't kissed me last night. He was thinking about Reema.

"Absolutely not. Don't even think like that. He's into you. Just wait. I bet you'll hear from him today. He was smitten."

I wasn't convinced. "We'll see. I'm going for a walk."

△ △ △ △

As I strolled around the campus, I tried to focus on creature watching and the intricate architecture of the old Tudor-style class buildings to keep my mind off of Oliver. There was a small group of Fae practicing their shape shifting on the lawn in front of the gymnasium, each one's power and beauty more glorious than the previous. Then, in the front windows of the Magical Arts building, witches were taking turns using fire or winds to do their bidding.

I frowned. I may have been half-Faerie and half-Vampire, but I didn't have any cool abilities like they did. I mean, the compulsion thing was interesting, but it was insanely hard to master, and I certainly couldn't turn into an animal or light things on fire. I continued walking, feeling slightly jealous but I was thankful for any feeling other than panic that I had somehow ruined my chances with Oliver.

But seriously, Reema? I didn't get it. When we were together it was as if the world was at peace. Like we were meant to be there in that moment, holding hands, allowing our lips to meet...I shook off the thought. Instead, I spiraled and let my mind picture Oliver and Reema "studying". Her hypnotic brown eyes pulling him in. His perfect face focused solely on her full red lips...

"Are you going to order something?" A soft feminine voice broke through my nightmare. Thank the gods.

I blinked and realized I was standing at the window of the coffee truck parked outside of the library. A girl with pointed ears and long canines tapped her sharp nails on the counter and stared at me as if I had two heads. Not that that would be abnormal there.

"Miss?"

"I'm so sorry. Yes, I'll have a type B mocha cappuccino." Unlike Bloody Goode's, the drinks on campus actually offered the ingredients that were promised via the beverages' nomenclature.

The girl nodded and got to work on my coffee. All of my overthinking had me parched. I took my fix of blood and caffeine and settled onto a bench nearby. I drew a long sip savoring the flavors when my pocket vibrated.

I reached for my phone and couldn't help but smile when I read the texts from Oliver on the screen. My heart flipped.

I just rode by Mama's Place and thought of you.

Dinner tomorrow night?

Chapter 8

"You look. Stunning." Oliver gave a shy half-smile as he looked me over in my orange sweater dress and knee-high brown suede boots, then immediately stared at the floor. I left my long blonde hair loose and it cascaded down my back. I bashfully swiped it from my shoulders as I gave him a onceover. Oliver was wearing a black button-down shirt with jeans, and his sleeves were rolled up to his forearms showing off his tanned skin. It was a simple and casual choice but somehow, he made it look incredible.

"Thank you. You look great too." I wasn't as nervous as I had been the first night we met, but a warm flush crept up my neck and filled my cheeks. I tucked a loose strand of hair behind my ear. I had suggested Luigi's for dinner, and we grabbed a table near the back.

Oliver seemed to be toiling over something and looked anxious, tapping his foot so violently that the table wobbled. As if realizing the earthquake, he was causing, he stopped tapping and gripped the sides of the table in his hands. "Sorry. Cali, I just wanted to apologize for the other night. I was...nervous." He tentatively raised his deep brown eyes to meet mine, but I could sense that he wasn't telling me everything.

I ignored my suspicion. "Don't worry about it." I smiled and he visibly relaxed and picked up a menu. I glanced at mine, but I couldn't get the image of him and Reema from my head. I had to know what he thought about her.

If he thought about her.

I really didn't want to play sloppy seconds. "So. I think you're tutoring my roommate. Reema?" I kept my eyes on the menu to look as nonchalant as possible.

"Oh yeah. She's your roommate? What a coincidence." He innocently smiled.

I raised an eyebrow. Coincidence indeed. "I guess you're musically talented *and* smart?"

He shrugged, "I don't know how 'smart' I am, but I'm good at sciences. I think that's why my mom is so hell-bent on the whole Pre-Med thing."

"That makes sense."

"What about you?" Oliver rested his chin on his hand, completely focused on me. It was intimidating.

"What about me?"

"What are you good at? Do you have any hidden talents I should know about?"

Besides stalking people and having uncontrollable lust for blood? I froze for a moment. "Um, well, I guess I'm decent at art."

He laughed. Still the most perfect sound I had ever heard. "Only 'decent'?"

I held my hands up and shrugged my shoulders.

"Do you draw? Paint? What's your medium of choice?"

"Paint. Ok, don't laugh, but I used to love watching Bob Ross on TV as a kid. I guess his 'happy trees' inspired me." I shifted my gaze trying to return to the pleasant memories of painting on the first canvases that my dad set up for me in the spiral tower of the castle. I had imagined that I was just like Rapunzel, minus the whole "being kidnapped and hidden away from everyone" part. When I looked back at Oliver, he was watching me, a half-smile on his face.

"Where'd you go? Thinking of Bob? Should I be jealous?"

I laughed so hard that I almost spit out the sip of water I had just taken. "I told you not to make fun of me!"

"Actually, you said not to laugh. I'm pretty sure making fun of you wasn't mentioned."

I narrowed my eyes at him, pretending to be offended, then smiled playfully. "Fair enough. And how are you going to be jealous of Bob Ross?"

His smile lit up the darkened corner of the restaurant we were sitting in. "I'd be jealous of anyone else who you showed interest in." He stared at me for a moment. "Seriously, though. How is it that you don't have a boyfriend? Or tons of them? Wait, you don't have tons of them...right?"

I laughed whole-heartedly again, and my cheeks were hot from blushing at his last statement. "No, I do not have tons of boyfriends. Or one." I shrugged, leaning back in my chair. "I guess I haven't really had much luck with dating. The last few guys I dated were either liars or cheaters. Or both."

Vampires weren't exactly the most trustworthy of creatures. That factoid made me happy to be only half-vamp. The Fae side of me kept me honest because they couldn't lie.

It kept me honest enough, anyway.

Oliver nodded as if he were recalling similar experiences in his own past relationships. "They must have been insane." He shyly moved his hand across the table and gingerly placed it over mine, intertwining our fingers.

My face flushed once more. If this date ended the same way as our last, I was definitely going to need a cold shower.

▲ ▲ ▲ ▲

After we had our fill of pasta and wine, we decided to walk down to Bloody Goode's to watch the live band that was playing at the bar. Oliver held my hand the whole way, this time taking mine in his as if we had been together for years. There was no pause. No nervousness. It just felt natural.

He was talking about his lacrosse game the week before when we strolled past an antique bookstore. I pulled him to a stop near the storefront. "Want to take a look? I know how much you love to read."

Shit. *Why did I say that?*

Oliver cocked his head to the side and his eyes narrowed slightly. I froze and my mouth went dry. I needed to hide the fact that I'd been watching him from behind the veil.

"Uh...I mean, I remember you telling me about your favorite books last time we hung out. They have some incredible first editions in this store."

"Right. I'm surprised you remembered." He grinned and led me inside the shop.

I exhaled, finally able to breathe again. I rolled my eyes to myself as I followed him through the revolving door.

How did stalkers keep from blowing their cover? Not that I was admitting to stalking Oliver. It was truly just close monitoring. If that.

The bookstore reeked of old paper and must and the smell was like heaven to me. Oliver also seemed to be on cloud-nine as we stalked up and down the wooden shelves that stretched almost to the ceiling. It was a small building, and every inch was filled to the brim with books. Old and loved, new and shiny, and all waiting patiently to be chosen by a lucky reader.

Oliver's eyes brightened as he surveyed the tower of first edition texts, and he brushed his fingers along the spines of the books as we slowly passed. He gripped tighter to my hand and led me toward the back of the store where there was a large stone fireplace with two armchairs and a loveseat that faced a roaring fire.

He took a seat on the loveseat, and I sat next to him, suddenly as anxious as I had been when we met. I glanced around for any glasses of liquid that I should've avoided. We were quiet for a bit before Oliver turned to face me.

"Calina, you are so...amazing," he stammered, "beautiful. Funny. I've never met anyone like you. There's something about you that just feels...different."

If he only knew.

He lifted my hand and brushed his lips against my knuckles. "Thank you for coming out with me again tonight. I thought for sure I blew it." He let out a low embarrassed laugh. "I should have just kissed you..."

Oliver's eyes glowed like amber as he intently stared into mine. My breathing grew ragged, and I bit down on my lower lip to keep it from trembling. He let go of my hand, placing his on my knee and leaned toward me, his gaze shifting to my lips and heaving chest then back to my eyes.

I heard his heart beating faster and could practically smell the blood that was surging through his veins. I swallowed, this time trying to overcome the feral need to taste it. To taste him. I licked my lips now and my hands gripped his arms as I pulled him closer. His hand slid further up my leg before moving them to my waist, moving closer to me on the loveseat.

His lips barely brushed past mine and he gently kissed my cheek then down along my neck. I nuzzled my face into his neck, the pulsation of his vessels intoxicating. I took in a deep breath, inhaling him, my fangs ready to make a fashionable entrance.

I had to stop.

Stop, Calina.

I considered pushing him gently away, fighting my own instinct of the predator I was. Then, he pulled me that much closer, kissing my jaw line, moving toward my mouth.

Screw it.

I clutched his shoulders, and my lips grazed his neck and then...

We both froze for a millisecond as the tips of my fangs barely pierced his skin. I immediately retracted my teeth, returning to my senses. It was like I had a momentary out of body experience. That millisecond felt like an eternity, as I waited for him to call me a psycho and take off running.

But he didn't. Instead, he emitted a low moan and his fingers grasped tighter to my hips and he softly kissed my neck once more. I allowed myself to get completely swept away in the moment and as his lips were about to land on mine, a loud pop, and a huge flame akin to a mini explosion burst outward from the fireplace, causing us both to jolt out of the loveseat to avoid being blasted by the flying sparks.

Oliver's eyes widened as he stared at the ash scattered along the stone between the fireplace and the chairs. One of the arms of the chairs was aflame, and he rushed to pat it out with his shoe. He looked shocked. No, terrified. Like it was somehow his fault.

"I'm sorry." He gazed down at the floor and burnt chair again then back to me, searching my face, my arms, as if looking for any injuries. "Are you hurt?"

"No, I'm ok."

"I'm sorry," he repeated. He wouldn't meet my eye and shoved a hand through his hair, clearly in his head about something.

"Hey. It's not your fault." His lips formed a tight line and at that moment, I really wished I could read minds like Shani. It was as if he was arguing with some thought in his mind. I reached over and took his hand, his palm slick with sweat. "Hey." I forced him to look at me. "It's ok. Come on, let's go to the bar."

He nodded and let me lead the way. I smiled back at him. "Probably shouldn't mention that little incident to the owner on our way out," I joked.

After all, it was just an accident.

Wasn't it?

Chapter 9

"Deep breaths." Ms. Dunning took a long inhale through her nose and let it out slowly through her perfectly shaped lips. "That's right. In...and out...," she drawled.

I squeezed my eyes shut, trying to concentrate on my deep breathing. *In...out...in...what the hell happened last night?*

Fires popped and sparked all the time. Okay, the near explosion was unexpected, but not completely crazy. I couldn't understand why he was so upset by it. I mean, sure, getting interrupted while making out kind of sucked, but he seemed scared. I suddenly thought back to what had happened that first night. We had almost kissed right before a random windstorm had Oliver so unhinged that he changed his mind. And he had that same expression on his face. Was it confusion, fear...guilt? It made no sense.

Or did it?

Wind...fire...

"Enjoying your daydream, Miss Strovsky?" Ms. Dunning's smooth voice brought me back to the present. She was standing in front of my desk, looking from me to the black crow that was perched before me. "You have to practice this. If you are not present enough to control your own mind, how do you expect to control the animal's?" She tsked and walked to the front of the room.

I looked down at the bird. "Sorry. I'm terrible at this." I heaved a sigh and the crow cawed in response.

"Ok everyone. That's enough for today." Ms. Dunning clapped her hands once and the crows on each of our tables flew in unison out of the open back window. "Next week, we will practice this on a more complex animal, so please practice your gifts in your free time." She made sure to make eye contact with me with that statement. "Dismissed."

I was almost safely out of the room and Ms. Dunning's guilt trip when she called me back. "Miss Strovsky, I would like to speak with you for a moment."

Bracing myself, I backed into the classroom and approached her desk. "Yes, ma'am?"

She gave me a pitying glance. "You know, I taught your mother back when she attended college here. She was such a talented young Moro." Ms. Dunning paused, something like regret in those beautiful features. "I expected so much more from her daughter."

"I know. I promise to practice more and leave my distractions outside of the classroom from now on."

"I hope you mean that. I am sure you do not want to take this course again in the Spring."

"No ma'am."

"Good. Then we will begin next week."

What? "I'm sorry?"

Ms. Dunning casually arranged a loose stack of papers on the mahogany desk she sat behind. "Your practice. I would like you to meet with me for tutoring outside of lecture." She stared at me point blank and I felt a slight pull of her compulsion. "This is not a request."

I focused on a spot on the floor to avoid her glare. "Yes, ma'am, I understand. I will see you after your lecture next week."

▲▲▲▲

"What you're suggesting is impossible." Shani dabbed at the layer of lipstick she had just applied. "If Oliver could use elemental magic, then he would know it. Have some relative that was a creature. Humans just don't...become magical. Besides, wouldn't we have sensed that he was supernatural?"

After fretting about my Vampire Arts class all afternoon, talking about my suspicions of Oliver's potential power was a welcome break.

"I guess. But what about the winds and flames when he was nervous and..." I lowered my voice to almost a whisper, "...and turned on?"

Shani spun so quickly in her chair that I stepped back in surprise. "What was that last part?" She had a mischievous grin spread over her now plum-colored lips.

I blushed and sat on the bed, staring at my hands. "We may have made out. A little." I sat up straighter and held up a finger to make a point, "But we still haven't officially kissed on the lips." As if that was helping me sound more innocent.

"Naughty girl. I'm so proud of you." She winked at me and went back to making up her face.

I cringed remembering how I let my blood lust get the best of me. Shani didn't need to know that part.

"Oh my gods, you *bit* him?" Shani was facing me once more, her mouth practically touching the floor. "Cali! What did he say? Did he freak out?"

I should have known she couldn't keep out of my thoughts. "Actually, he just kind of...went with it." I shrugged, needing to change the subject as quickly as possible. "Anyway, my theory. The wind and fire thing, and remember how I thought he could see me somehow from behind the veil? Oh! And he doesn't really remember his father...so...it's possible."

Shani pursed her lips. "Circumstantial at best."

I rolled my eyes. "I thought you were an Econ major. Not Pre-Law."

"You're one to talk, Miss 'I Need Vampire Tutoring'."

I glared at her. Of course she already knew that I was failing without me telling her.

Shani sighed, "All I'm saying is that we need more proof. You've got to tell him."

"Tell him what, exactly?" I asked, although I knew what she was referring to.

She raised her eyebrows, smirking. "I think you know."

"How will that help give us proof? This is about Oliver possibly being...different. This has nothing to do with me."

"Not technically, but if he is truly experiencing this magic and he has no idea why, he might want to know that he's not alone. That what he's going through is real and not some figment of his imagination."

Shani was right. If there was any validity to my gut feeling, then Oliver just might be more accepting of my truth if he's got a secret too. But if I was wrong...

Shani reached for my hand and squeezed. "Let's just hope you aren't."

▲▲▲▲

I was waiting impatiently for Oliver on the old wooden bridge in the center of town. I wrung my hands together and paced back and forth several times. What the heck was I doing? I couldn't tell him that I was a vampire. He'd think I was nuts. Even if he did have some kind of unknown magic, there was no way this was going to be a believable fact.

I jumped at the hand touching my elbow, bringing my pacing to a stop. I turned to see Oliver standing in front of me, his smile lighting up his entire face and wavy brown hair glinting in the sunlight. My heart sank. Another reason for him to think I'm crazy. Most humans believed we couldn't go out in the daylight. It was just another myth made up for Hollywood.

Oliver's gentle smile faded, now muted by the look of concern in his eyes. "Are you ok?"

No.

Ugh, this was going to suck. I pulled my arm out of his warm hand and my gaze shifted out to the calm waters of the river below. "Oliver...," I started, "about what happened last night..."

He immediately inched toward me and took my elbow in his hand, turning me to face him. "I'm so sorry. I have no idea what happened with the fire." He furrowed his brow and thrust his hands in his pockets, rocking back on his heels. "And I don't know why I reacted like that...and the other night...it was like this weird feeling..." He looked me dead in the eye now, his breath catching a bit as if he wanted me to respond then changed his mind. He looked away. "I don't know what I'm saying. I'm sorry for acting so off. I just get nervous around you, I guess."

I peered out to the river once more and the water seemed to be flowing faster, cresting repeatedly as if an incoming storm were moving the currents. My brow furrowed at the churning waters and wondered if just *maybe*...I glanced at Oliver.

He flashed that beautiful smile at me, and I melted.

No. Stay strong. Eventually, he would have to learn the truth about me. Better now before I got too attached. Well, more attached.

I steeled myself. "No, it's not about the other night. Oliver, I have something to tell you. You know how I, kind of, bit you?" I closed my eyes briefly and cleared my dry throat. I was going to be sick.

His lips curled up on one side and he raised an eyebrow. "Yeah. It was kinky."

I sighed internally. Boys. "Yeah. Right, well, it wasn't intentional. It was more or less an instinct." I searched his face and could see the questions already forming in his brain. Ok, new tactic. "Ok, so you know how you said you were just feeling 'off' and couldn't explain your reaction the other night?"

He nodded, his smile now gone and his lips forming a tight line.

"Oliver, I think you…you are experiencing some magic." I swallowed hard. Just rip off the band-aid. "And I know it sounds crazy. But I think this might be true because I also have some…magic." I heaved a sigh. I wasn't making any sense.

He opened his mouth to speak, and I held up my hand. "I'm a vampire. Well, half-vampire. I guess the other half is Fae?" My stomach roiled and I held his gaze watching every fear I had about telling him flash through his brown eyes.

"You're a vampire." It wasn't a question. Oliver nodded once in resignation. "You're a vampire. Who likes garlic and is currently not bursting into flames in the middle of the day." He leaned on the stone wall of the bridge and stared out to the water. The waves looked as if they could topple a cruise ship.

I reached tentatively for his forearm, and he turned on me so quickly, I jerked my hand away and stepped back.

Oliver shoved his hands in his pockets and wouldn't make eye contact with me. "You know, if you weren't into me, you could have just said so. But making up some kind of crazy lie?" He finally locked eyes with me. "I thought you were different."

"I am. Just not in the way you thought." I made sure to keep holding his gaze. I wanted him to see in my face that I was telling him the truth. "Oliver, I know how it sounds, but I'm not making this up. And I am not trying to push you away." I edged closer to him, but he backed away from me, disgusted, as if I was a leper. "Please. You have to believe me."

I held my breath and waited for the worst. Waited for some laughing or more yelling and the "You're insane" commentary. But it never came.

Instead, he shook his head slightly as if he was fighting his own thoughts, and disappointment settled over his features. Then, without another word, he simply turned and walked away from me, leaving me alone on the bridge above the violent and raging river.

Chapter 10

I had never been more excited for a full moon than I was that weekend. I hadn't heard from Oliver for almost a week, and I didn't expect to hear from him ever again. The entire situation was why it was frowned upon for creatures to bother with humans as love interests. It never ended pretty. Just look at what happened to Frankenstein's monster. All he wanted was to be accepted, and how did the town's people respond? They tore him to bits with pitchforks.

Luckily my dad was his usual quiet self during dinner. He didn't even bug me about my lacking grades. I think he knew I wasn't in the mood to have that argument again. Maybe my not begging to join him on this season's Wild Hunt clued him in and warned him to leave a girl in peace.

I lay there on my bed that evening, not even wanting to look out the window to see if he was there, in his chair with his books. Ok, I wanted to, but I felt so ashamed of what had happened and what I was that I told myself it wasn't a good idea.

I wished Shani was there. I could've used a friend. And a drink.

Maybe just one tiny peek wouldn't hurt. Rolling up from my bed, I tiptoed to my window and rested my forehead on the pane. Of course, he was there, content in his own little world he traveled to through the pages of his books.

Why had I ruined everything?

I closed my eyes preventing an onslaught of tears and when I opened them, Oliver was standing by the railing of his deck staring at me. He waved his hand, his phone held up, motioning for me to grab mine.

I blinked. I knew it. I knew he had seen me the other night. I pulled my phone from my pocket, and it vibrated in my palm, the call from Oliver coming in through the veil. Another impossibility somehow possible.

Suddenly worried I was hallucinating the whole thing, I tentatively answered, still watching him through the window.

"How can I see you?" was all he asked.

I didn't respond.

He asked again, "How can I see you when I know nothing should be there but a mountain range. There should be mountains and trees and night but now...there's this castle? And I've seen you before. Standing there in the window, I mean. I need to know how."

"Because you are like me."

Oliver didn't say anything more. Just nodded slightly and hung up the phone. I watched as he looked up at the cloudless night sky as raindrops began to sprinkle down on his head from seemingly nowhere.

My phone vibrated again, and I put it up to my ear. "Oli—"

"I need you to show me."

▲▲▲▲

The only way to prove to Oliver that what I had told him was true was to bring him to St. Anne's. Sure, there were a few places in town that only creatures could venture, but seeing me in my element, meeting my friends, that seemed like the best bet.

Of course, that meant outing Shani and Reema too.

"It's the only way, Shani." I pleaded with my best friend while sitting on our favorite bench between classes. "I need your help. I think he knows that there's something different about himself. Just think about the wonderful service you'd be providing to another creature?" I pouted my lips out and gave her my best puppy-dog eyes.

Shani crossed her arms over her chest. "Fine. But only Oliver and only because he needs help. We can't just go around letting random humans in on a secret that's been kept since the beginning of time."

I threw my arms around her, squeezing her in a tight hug. "Thank you!"

She didn't return my embrace. "Reema is not going to like it. Not that I care." She giggled and leaned into me. "When can we expect our guest?"

"Tomorrow afternoon." I hugged her a bit tighter. "Also, I need to borrow your Gucci boots."

Shani jerked away from me. "Seriously?"

"Pretty please?"

She sighed. "Man, you really owe me for this."

▲ ▲ ▲ ▲

For the first time since I laid eyes on Oliver from behind the veil, I didn't have an ounce of anxiety. I was excited. I had never shared my creature self with someone from the human world.

Truthfully, I had never shared much of my entire self to anyone other than Shani.

I regressed back to being terrified.

I walked up to where Oliver was leaning against a streetlamp along the old bridge, his face completely unreadable. No easy smile or even a gleam in those eyes. Just a mask of cold stoicism. His arms were crossed resolutely against his brown suede jacket as if he were intentionally blocking out anything that might upset his belief system. This was going to be harder than I thought.

He pushed himself away from the lamp and came toward me with his hands in his jean pockets. "I might have agreed to come here, but this doesn't mean I believe you."

I stopped and let him meet me where I stood and tilted my head. "Hello to you too. And I know it all sounds like something you'd see on a bad cable channel, but I'm telling the truth." I stared at my feet. No. Stay confident. Seeing was believing.

I jerked my chin to the right where my car was parked. "I'll show you." He simply nodded and let me lead the way. I wasn't about to *walk* him through the valley. That would be crazy.

Oliver was silent for the entire drive, and I could feel him tense as we left the city and drove down the hills and deeper into the woods.

At first glance, the pine forest on the outskirts of the valley seemed pretty normal. A few evergreens here, broken tree stumps there. But if you kept making your way through toward the Academy, that was when the definition of "normal" changed.

I had to slow for a unicorn that raced in front of us. I turned quickly to see Oliver's reaction to seeing one of the most mythical beasts in history, but he was staring out the other window, completely oblivious to the magical elements all around us.

My shoulders sagged. So much for an opportunity to help prove my case that the paranormal was, in fact, normal.

I rolled my eyes and kept driving. The dense forest thinned out, and I knew we were close. "We're almost there."

"I didn't realize St. Anne's was so far out." Oliver glanced at me, his eyes widening slightly, and I wondered if he was suddenly thinking I was taking him into the woods to murder him. Seemed plausible as someone you just met told you she was a vampire and was now driving you to the middle of nowhere.

I attempted a smile to help him relax. I even tried a little compulsion to give him some calm thoughts, focusing my eyes on his, widening and narrowing them.

"Why are you looking at me like that?" His brow furrowed and he went back to staring out his window.

I grimaced. I really should have practiced that more.

I let out a breath as we neared the open expanse of St. Anne's Academy. Finally. That thirty-minute drive felt like five months. "We're here." I drove down the long drive, buffered by the ancient oak trees layered with Spanish moss. "This is St. Anne's." I smiled up at the tree-lined path of prestige.

Oliver leaned forward in his seat, looking wide-eyed at the beautiful college campus that everyone had heard about, but somehow usually forgot existed soon after.

Which wasn't a coincidence. St. Anne's liked its exclusivity, and if humans forgot its existence, they wouldn't try to apply. Or ask questions about the strange location and student body. So, why not a spell to make them forget they had ever heard of our small college? You had to love magic.

"This is..." His voice trailed off and he sat back in the seat. He turned to me, finally a half-smile on his face, giving me hope. "Definitely not what I expected." His smile disappeared and he crossed his arms. "But just because the Academy is kind of hidden out here, it still proves nothing. St. Anne's isn't a secret or anything."

I shook my head in response and parked the car near the administration building. "Come on. There's a lot to see."

I led Oliver around the grounds of the old Tudor-style building, stopping at the fountain in the middle of the quad where Shani and I always met between our classes. He appeared to be in awe of the architecture, but there was still skepticism in his eyes. I needed to show him some of the magic.

And, yes, I could have just shown him my fangs and had a dog bring me a beer through compulsion, but where was the fun in that? Plus, he didn't ask me to. Maybe he wasn't quite ready to have that image of me yet.

I wasn't ready for Oliver to have that image of me either.

"Shani will be here in just a minute." I took a seat on the bench and motioned for him to sit next to me. "Her Econ class should be over soon."

"Econ? No special Potions or Blood Sucking 101?"

He was mocking me. "Ha. Actually, those courses are offered. Maybe not the Blood Sucking, but Vampire Arts, yes."

He opened his mouth to say something then closed it again, his lips now forming a tight line, trying so hard to keep a closed mind. He leaned his arms on his knees and tapped his foot impatiently. "I don't know why I came here. This is dumb."

"Hi!" Shani's voice rang through the air, and her long bohemian style skirt swished and swayed as she sauntered up to us.

Thank the gods.

She smiled at Oliver, and he stood to greet her. She spread her arms wide, gesturing to our surroundings. "Welcome to the proverbial 'other side of the tracks'. Calina told me that you now know some privy information." She looked at me then back to Oliver.

"She shared some unbelievable information. I mean, I'm just..." he glanced at me, a flicker of pain in his eyes that was gone in an instant, "...I'm having a hard time believing that this isn't a very elaborate lie." He looked back at Shani. "Are you a vampire too?"

The bite was back in his voice and Shani just smiled. "Gods, no!" She reached for his hand. "May I?"

He nodded and allowed her to take his hands in both of hers. She closed her eyes and took a deep inhale. As she exhaled, eyes still shut, Oliver's look of confusion rapidly changed into one of fear and shock and his eyes darted all around them as if he were seeing something that wasn't visible to me.

I bit down on my lower lip watching the panic worsen in his eyes and gusts of wind began to swirl all around me, causing my knee-length skirt to blow uncomfortably high. I held it down to my legs as the gusts strengthened with every passing second. His heart was beating wildly in his chest, and I tensed, hoping Oliver didn't inadvertently cause a tornado.

Suddenly, Oliver screamed, "Stop!", and yanked his hands from Shani's. The wind stopped immediately too, and he backed away, panting, from Shani. His hands went to his forehead, and he looked all around as if he were just transported from some other universe to the place in which he stood before staring daggers at her. "What the hell did you just do to me?"

She shrugged with one shoulder and a smirk. "Just a little chaos."

I glared at her for a moment. Couldn't she have just read his thoughts instead of scaring him half to death?

Oliver was still staring at Shani in disbelief. "I was...there was...it was like I was in a different world. I was being chased." His eyes narrowed. "How did you do that?"

"It's just one of my powers. I'm not a vampire. My dad is Set." She shrugged. "The god, Set." Shani examined her nails as if the fact that she was a demigod was commonplace. "Basically, I can change your surroundings and force you into an environment of my designing. That one was a scary one. Sorry." She smiled innocently.

Oliver didn't say anything, and he had a faraway look in his eyes. Maybe he was just trying to process. Maybe he was trying to remember how we got here so he could run away as fast as he could.

Finally, he glanced in my direction with an eyebrow raised and allowed a nervous chuckle escape. "She's a demigod." Then, as if on cue, a pack of werewolves were taking a group run while practicing their phasing in and out of human form. His eyes grew about three sizes, and he simply raised a pointed finger in the track team's direction. "They are wolves...but...not?"

I nodded and gave him a half-smile. "Are you ok?" He looked like he might have a mental breakdown at any moment.

"I mean, sure. Everything I thought I knew about my world was a complete lie. But, yeah, I'm ok." Oliver paced back and forth in the small space near the bench, mumbling to himself. "There's a college that produces some of the most successful people in the world that everyone just sort of forgets about...ancient gods are a thing...wolves apparently can be humans at the same time...and you're a..." He stopped pacing and stared me dead in the eye. "You're a vampire?" The statement came out as a question, as if he were just realizing it at that very moment.

Shani gazed at me, and I wondered if she was worried that he might be teetering on the side of going crazy too.

"Yes." That was all that I could muster. I suddenly felt ashamed of myself. "I mean, I'm half-vampire. Half Fae," I added as if that somehow made it better, staring at the ground and not meeting his eye.

"But the sunlight and garlic...and sleeping in a coffin?"

"All fiction. Humans had to make vampires sound much scarier than we actually are for Hollywood. I definitely don't sleep in a coffin. I'm super claustrophobic." I paused for a moment, then said in a much lower tone, "The blood drinking thing is true." I shyly glanced at him from under my eyelashes.

To my astonishment, Oliver wasn't fazed by my comment about my dietary preferences and continued his line of questioning. "Are you immortal then?"

"No. I mean, I don't think so. I will most likely have a much longer lifespan than a human...but I won't live forever. That is another myth created by humans. There's a silver lining, though; I will get a pretty good set-up in the afterlife at my dad's."

Oliver lips formed a tight line. "Mmhmm. You told me you have some kind of magic?"

"It's nowhere near as cool as Shani's, but, yes, I can use compulsion. I'm not very good at it though. On people anyway. And most animals." I continued to study the ground. "Oh, and I can go behind the veil. To my dad's house."

"Her dad is the Erlking." Shani was now standing next to me and placed a hand on my shoulder. She must have read my thoughts. I wasn't mad at it.

Oliver gave a sideways glance at Shani after her statement about my dad, then returned to pacing.

"I know it's a lot to take in. But you wanted me to show you."

He ignored my comment. "That's where I saw you then. You were behind the veil." He stopped in place, then slowly sat back down on the bench. The weight of the truth must have hit him like a ton of bricks. He rested his head in his hands. "But how? How did I see you? The veil doesn't..." he sighed, "...didn't exist." His eyes met mine, a strange sadness in them.

I sat down next to him and tentatively took his hand in mine, half-expecting him to pull away. But he didn't. Warmth filled my cheeks. "There's more." I winced when his face shot up from his hands to look at me, fear and disbelief in his beautiful brown eyes.

"I think you can control the elements. That's why strange things happen to you when you get. Well, nervous or...excited." His hand gripped mine a little tighter.

Shani took a seat on the other side of Oliver. "That's probably the reason that you can see through the veil."

It took several moments for him to take in this new information. "So, the wind and the fire?"

"Both elements. So is earth and water, which explains the rain the other night, and the water beneath the bridge when I told you about. Well, about all of this." I gestured to the expansive campus of creatures.

"Where did they...you. Where did you all come from? Why here?"

I shrugged. "Freyshire, mostly, but I'm sure that isn't the only place where creatures live. It just happens to neighbor one of the most prestigious colleges where we can go to fully come into our powers. But even then, not everyone comes here. I'm sure several attend Freyshire College with you."

"So, there are more...," he cleared his throat, "more 'people' like you? Out in town, I mean. And humans have no idea?"

I nodded and raised a shoulder. "I don't think they have really looked for us since they've always believed that creatures don't exist."

"Right." Oliver's brow furrowed and he stared absently out to the fountain, the spraying waters changing from black to red and back again. The Aquatics Team had just begun their Wave Arts training and he nodded his chin toward them. "Water nymphs. Huh."

"Sirens, actually."

"Of course they are." He shook his head then lifted my hand to his lips, brushing a soft kiss against my fingers. "I'm sorry. For what I said the other night. Or didn't say."

I leaned my head on his shoulder and Shani threw her arm around his other shoulder, flanking him in an awkward creature sandwich.

Oliver rested his head on mine. "So now what?"

Chapter 11

I decided to drive Oliver home just after Shani and I walked him past the Fae shifters. I thought he may have been a bit overwhelmed by that point. I mean, I know I freaked out a little the first time I saw a person turn into an animal, so I could only imagine what he must have thought. Especially since the dragon shifters were joining in. There would be other times to show him more of the Academy.

I parked near the old bridge where we had met earlier that day and was about to ask him if he would want to see me again, when he pulled me into his arms. I was surprised by the embrace, but I allowed myself to fall into his warm and muscular chest.

He rested his chin in the space between my neck and shoulder. "I didn't want to believe you."

"I know. It's kind of impossible to believe that there are creatures roaming around." I tightened my grip around his waist, breathing in his scent. Pine tar and cloves. He was like a walking, talking Christmas store.

He gently pulled away but kept his hands resting on my hips. "That's not why I was hesitant. I think...I think I was hoping you were lying so I didn't have to accept that something's wrong with me." His voice wavered and he rested his forehead on mine. "The fire and wind...I've had weird things like that happen around me before."

I took his face in my hands. "There is nothing wrong with you. You might be able to control the elements. If anything, that makes you incredible."

Oliver sighed. "So, I'm a witch? A faerie?"

"I don't know yet. But I'll be here to help you figure it out."

He kissed my forehead. "Thank you for today."

"Thank you for letting me show you, well...me."

The simple smile that I liked so much played at his lips, his sharp cheekbones and sole dimple making my breath catch in my throat.

"I want to know so much more about you. And, I guess, me too?" his brown eyes shined like copper reflecting hues of burnt sienna and orange under the setting sun.

I desperately wanted to kiss him. Forever.

"Come and watch me play tomorrow night? Then maybe we can get some food and you can tell me more about this elemental magic thing?"

I leaned closer and placed a kiss on his cheek. "Can't wait."

The next night, I put on my cutest romper and strappy gold wedge sandals that gave me legs for days. It was an exceptionally warm evening for October, and Shani and I walked arm in arm to Bloody Goode's to watch Oliver play.

"Hey bitches." A high-pitched saccharine voice pierced the air behind us in the line getting into the bar.

I crossed my arms over my chest and side eyed Shani.

"What? I didn't tell her about tonight! I swear."

We both turned and I attempted a smile, but it probably looked more like an annoyed smirk. "Reema. Good to see you."

Reema beamed, her perfectly white teeth sparkling under the fairy lights lined along the awning. She looked like a superstar in her tiny leather mini skirt and black oversized sweater. She leaned in and gave us both air kisses on our cheeks, then said in an overly sweet tone, "Well, someone had to come and supervise you two after your little secret sharing yesterday."

I cocked my head in feigned confusion. "I have no idea what you're talking about."

"Please, Calina. I am one of Set's daughters too. I can read minds just like Shani." Reema eyed her half-sister. "Probably better. Anyway, last night, I settled into my tutoring session with Oliver, and you know what was on his mind?" She paused a second with her hands on her hips, and when neither of us guessed, she continued. "Well, it wasn't my amazing body, that's for sure. All that boy could think about was how many creatures he might have met in Freyshire without realizing what they really were." Her sugary tone was gone, and she stared daggers at me and Shani.

I silently thanked the gods he was thinking about *anything* else but her body.

"Don't worry, he only saw the school and some of what Cali and I can do. No one mentioned you or gave you a second thought." Shani pursed her lips. "You should be used to that." She walked toward an outdoor table next to the makeshift stage and we trailed behind her.

Reema appeared absolutely livid, but she joined us at the front table anyway. We ordered drinks and I waited impatiently for Oliver to take the stage. The tension at our table was palpable. I knew she'd be pissed, but she would forgive us, eventually, and it wasn't like we told him about her. Not directly, anyway. He knew that Reema was my roommate, but hopefully he was too distracted by the life-changing information that was forced upon him to put two and two together.

Then again, maybe I should have reminded Oliver that Reema was my roommate. He may have been too nervous to be alone with her and not want to tutor her anymore.

Reema's eyes were cold and calculated and she held my gaze for a brief instance. A shudder went down my spine. Shit. She was probably listening to my every thought right now.

I stared right back at her, daring her to keep reading me.

Baaabbyy shark do do do...

She sneered at me and took a swig of her drink. I just laughed and turned to face the stage when I heard the manager announce Oliver. His lips curved up slightly until his dimple made an appearance when he saw me in the crowd. He was wearing all black except for his brown jacket that he wore so well, and he kept me in his sights as he took his place on the stage.

Every time I laid eyes on Oliver's perfect face, I could have sworn that he became that much more beautiful. I was so used to watching, *not* stalking, him through my window, daydreaming of one day meeting him. And now, when his eyes landed on mine and that crooked grin lit up his face and the entire town of Freyshire, I was actually surprised.

I couldn't quite believe it. He liked *me.* Even though he knew that I wasn't...normal. Even when he knew that I craved a little blood now and then. He liked me anyway.

He continued to watch me from the stage as he started to play, and I realized he was singing to me. Color flooded his cheeks and his eyes flickered under the lights. I was drunk on the warm feeling rushing over me. I allowed the magic of his voice to whisk my mind away. Closing my eyes, I swayed along, letting the music flow through me.

Pop.

Pop pop pop.

My eyes shot open at the sound of glass exploding in a series of loud bangs. The tiny fairy lights that were strung above the patio popped and burst into small balls of fire, one after another, glass shards darting down into the crowd. People were panicking and ran indoors or onto the streets to avoid the falling glass, Reema and Shani among them.

I covered my head and ran to Oliver still on stage. He had stopped playing and his eyes were wide with fear. He looked at me, holding up his hand, wisps of smoke circling above his beet red fingertips. I gently touched them with my own fingers and jerked away at the burning heat radiating from his hand. "Are you ok? Your fingers are blazing hot!"

"I think...Calina, I *did* that." Oliver slowly got up from the stool. "I was just playing. I saw you and...the song. It was for you."

My heart fluttered and a slow smile began to spread across my lips. Then I noticed the fear in his eyes. *Ok, this isn't about you. Focus.* I swallowed my growing infatuation, nodding and waiting for him to continue.

He ran a hand through his hair. "My fingers felt like they were going to burst into flames and then." He gestured to the busted lights above.

I shrugged. "Oops?"

"Oops?! I just committed vandalism and don't even know how I did it!"

"I know. I'm sorry." I looked around at the broken glass and people were starting to come back onto the patio to assess what happened. "We should probably get out of here, though."

Oliver didn't say much as we walked down the dark alleyways and out to the old bridge. He stopped in the middle of the bridge and looked out into the churning black water below, leaning his forearms on the ancient gray brick railing. I sidled up next to him, mimicking his stance. I wanted to hold him and let him know that he was going to be ok, but I also hated to make promises that I wasn't sure I could keep.

The same hint of sadness that I had seen for the briefest moment the night we met flashed in his eyes as he stared silently into the night. "Remember last night, when I told you that this kind of *thing* has happened before?" His voice was barely a whisper. "I was four. My dad and I were at some park. I don't remember what was going on, but I know that I was upset. Throwing a tantrum about something. Then the winds. They were gusting like...like a hurricane or tornado. Stuff was blowing all over the place. There was trash from knocked over bins, leaves, and the swings were tossed over the rail that held them. I was just so upset, and I couldn't stop crying. Then it was like this wall of wind blasted over the whole park, knocking people to the ground and limbs from trees were thrown everywhere like missiles." Oliver paused a minute, wiping the palms of his hands over his eyes.

I realized that I was holding my breath. I somehow knew where he was going with this story. I reached over and took his hand in mine, leaning my shoulder on his.

He squeezed my hand in response. "I was thrown several feet into the parking lot from the blast. And when I was able to get up again, I didn't see my dad anywhere. Of course, I freaked out. I was just a toddler. I searched the park and spotted a group of people huddled together near the swing-set." Oliver's throat bobbed. "They said he was killed instantly. A large tree branch fell right on top of him."

I closed my eyes, feeling every ounce of his pain. "I'm so sorry, Oliver."

"It was my fault. And I didn't even realize it. Since then, there have been similar instances but not that intense. It's only when I get angry...or..." He looked at me. "Or when I feel something strongly. For someone."

A tear streamed down his face, shattering my heart. He turned away and wiped the evidence of his vulnerability from his cheek.

"What happened to your father was not your fault."

"How can you say that? If I had controlled myself..."

"You were a kid. You had no idea that you could wield elemental magic. How were you supposed to know that you were the cause of anything that happened around you on that day or since?"

He seemed to consider this, and I could see the wheels turning in his head, but he said nothing more on the subject and stared down at the water once more. "Have you always known? I mean, have you always been a vampire?"

"If you're asking if I was 'made' like on TV shows, then no. I was born this way. My mom is a full vampire, and she was born that way too."

Oliver turned toward me, leaning his hip on the stone railing. "Does it get easier? The whole 'being a creature' thing?"

I pondered how I should respond to his question. It had never really been easy, and there were aspects about being a vampire that truly sucked. No pun intended. I needed to be honest with him. If Oliver was going to learn to love this side of himself, he needed the truth about the good and bad of being a creature. "Easier isn't how I would describe it. But you will eventually learn how to make your powers work for you. And on the plus side, you've lived your life as a human for the last nineteen years, so there isn't much you'd have to do to convince everyone else in Freyshire that you're not."

"I guess that's a positive." He smiled, revealing his adorable dimple on his left cheek. His eyes flashed with a sudden sadness, and he furrowed his brow. "My mom never brings it up, you know. The weird things that happen around me. It's like she ignores it, or doesn't notice...is that possible?"

My heart broke all over again for him. This was not going to be an easy transition for him. "For her not to notice?"

He nodded.

"No. I mean, you saw how everyone at Bloody Goode's ran for cover. It's not like humans aren't affected by elemental magic. Then again, for someone who knows nothing about magic, they may seem like strange coincidences or bad luck." My answer didn't appear to console him at all. I wanted nothing more than to wrap my arms around him and protect him from the hurt that he had gone through and was bound to go through now that he knew the truth about himself.

Instead, I decided that just standing near him and allowing him time and space to process was the best comfort I could offer him.

"Are you happy? Being different, I mean."

I was surprised by Oliver's question. It was something I had never really asked myself. I shrugged my shoulders slightly,

"I've not really felt any different. I mean, I haven't known anything else. So, yes. I'm happy. I love who I am, where I come from. I'm not thrilled about the bloodlust thing but--"

"Bloodlust?" He shook his head. "I'm sorry, that's. You don't have to answer that."

I probably shouldn't have mentioned the bloodlust thing. I wasn't sure Oliver was ready to hear about my unusual craving. I sighed. There was no turning back now. "It's ok. Bloodlust is almost like a compulsion. An instinct so powerful that it can take over all of your senses and make you see red. When it hits...when it hits, my entire body burns, and it takes every ounce of my willpower to control myself and not tear into the throat of whatever random person who happens to be near me at the time."

Oliver's expression was unreadable. I gulped, immediately wishing I could rewind the last two minutes and steer the conversation away from my vampire impulses. I was so stupid. Why did I go into detail like that?

"Have you ever...?" He didn't finish his question, but I knew exactly what he wanted to ask me.

"Killed someone? No. I don't feed directly on humans, though sometimes it's tempting." That was putting it mildly.

A look of relief settled over Oliver's face, and I prayed that we could change the subject to something a little less violent. I waited for him to say something more, but he seemed content, for now at least, and circled back to face out to the water again.

We stood there in silence for a while, just watching the river ebb and flow below the bridge. I was happy to not be discussing vampirisms anymore, but my mind and emotions were still running a million miles an hour. Trying to think of how I could help Oliver learn to control his magic, thinking about what he said about his mom.

Then it hit me.

Suddenly it made sense. He had to have gotten his powers from someone and his father would have been able to recognize, and prevent, the worsening windstorm during Oliver's tantrum if his father had been a creature.

Maybe his mom *was* ignoring it. Keeping the truth from him. Because she knew what he was.

Because she was the same.

Chapter 12

B ut that was crazy. I had run Oliver's story about his magic and his father's untimely death over and over in my head about a million times since we said goodnight the evening before. I knew it was insane, but his mother being able to wield elemental powers just like her son made sense.

"But why would she keep it from Oliver? Especially after the accident with his dad? You would think that she would want him to learn to control his magic so something like that didn't happen again." Shani's voice came out of nowhere.

I jumped and whirled around on Shani who was leaning on my bedroom door frame. "Geez, Shani, you scared me. And that was supposed to be personal. Oliver told me about his dad in confidence."

Shani simply raised her eyebrows and made herself comfortable on the bed. "Sorry, but it's hard to ignore your thoughts when they've been practically screaming at me throughout the entire dorm."

I sat next to her, heaving a sigh of frustration.

"Are you going to say something to Oliver? About his mom, I mean?"

I wanted to. But without knowing if I was right, I couldn't go around accusing random people of being a witch. Or Fae. Or whatever he was. "No. I can't. I need to meet her and see for myself. I think I've given him enough to process over the past few days." I glanced at the time on my phone. "Besides, today is all about seeing what Oliver can do. I was able to convince Reema to ask her Elementals teacher, Dr. Winter, to work with us."

"Ok..."

"What?"

Shani gave me a sidelong glance. "That probably means that Reema is going to go with you."

I didn't think about that. Damn.

▲ ▲ ▲ ▲

I met Oliver at the edge of town around six o'clock that evening and drove us back down the valley to St. Anne's Academy. He was much more attentive to his surroundings during the drive now that he knew what to look for. Unfortunately, I still didn't get a chance to show him the elusive unicorn before we got deeper into the brush, but we did see a band of Gargoyles trudging along in the same direction as the school. It wasn't that big a deal. Just a bunch of security guards on their way to the College for their night shift.

Oliver, of course, was in awe. All of it was brand new to him, and now that he wasn't avoiding believing in the paranormal, he took in each and every detail during our drive through the forest.

The light had returned to his eyes and his smile that made me swoon was spread wide on his face. There wasn't a trace of the sadness or guilt that had plagued him last night on the bridge.

Now I really couldn't ask him about his mom.

As we slowly drove up the grand entrance to the school, I could hear Oliver's heart racing. I was about to reach for his hand and noticed he was looking out the window at the towering building ahead. I swallowed hard; my own breath ragged at seeing his jugular vein pulsing with such effort that it was practically calling out to me. I could even smell the blood rushing through his vessels. It was even more Christmas-y than the scent of his skin. Heat rushed through me, and it wasn't the sexy kind.

Gods. I was practically salivating. I bit down on my bottom lip hard, hoping to distract myself and subtly slow my breathing. But the blaze inside of me spread like wildfire, making my fingers and toes tingle and burn with wanting. My throat ached. His pulse thrummed like a beautifully delectable melody in my ears.

The aroma. The movement. I couldn't look away. I couldn't—

"Whoa, Cali, stop!"

Oliver's shout broke the bloodlust trance I must have been in, and I slammed the brakes, bringing the car to an immediate stop mere inches from the edge of the fountain in the middle of the quad. Soaking wet sirens poked their mossy heads from the water to see what the commotion was, and a couple of them threw me an angry hand gesture.

"Geez. Are you ok?" Oliver had one hand braced against the dashboard and the other on my arm as I gripped the steering wheel so tightly, my knuckles were white.

"I'm so sorry. I don't know what happened..." I let my voice trail off not wanting to share the fact that moments ago I had fantasized about draining every ounce of his blood. No wonder I was failing Vampire Arts. I couldn't even control myself around the guy I was in to.

Oliver sunk back against the seat and exhaled.

All I could muster was a murmur of another 'sorry' and backed the car into an actual parking spot.

▲▲▲▲

Oliver's heartbeat was humming in my ears again and he walked a step behind me when we entered the large greenhouse behind the Magical Arts building. I glanced behind me and gave him an encouraging smile.

He flashed me a brief smile in return but as his eyes darted all around the greenhouse, I knew he was anxious. Who wouldn't be? I mean, even I was overwhelmed and awed at the amazing gardens that surrounded us. The greenhouse was a building made up of only windows that covered all four walls. Each window was bordered with white steel beams that supported plant boxes along every window base. Vines and branches covered in white Yarrow and dark Nightshade berries climbed the walls all the way to the ceiling, and Venus Flytraps and Shame plants creeped along the stone paths that traced throughout the greenhouse.

Oliver stopped to inspect one of the Nightshade flowers popping up in its usual evening bloom. He reached out to touch its velvet leaves pushing from the ground, then paused as the plant jerked away from his touch. "It's like it's...alive. I mean, I know it's *living*, but, like it has a brain. It knows I want to touch it, and it doesn't want me to."

"Good. Nightshade flowers are deadly."

Oliver quickly retracted his hand and put both of them into his pockets.

"Ah, welcome. Welcome." Dr. Winter stood at a small planting table near the back of the greenhouse. He was elbow deep in soil but stopped whatever he was doing to acknowledge our presence.

Dr. Winter was an odd-looking Faerie. Most of their kind were stunningly beautiful. Tall. Muscular with angled features and luscious flowing hair. Not Dr. Winter. He was short and plump with a mop of silvering hair that was shaved short, barely brushing the tips of his elongated ears. His ears may have been the only telling sign of his Fae-dom, aside from his searing emerald eyes.

No, he didn't look like your average Fae. And he was definitely the winner in his marriage. Mrs. Winter was the chorus director at the Academy and also taught Algebra. She was tall and lean, and she was a tree nymph, so her glittering skin had the most gorgeous forest green glow.

Oliver had stopped walking at the sight of the little man, so I took his hand in mine and led the way.

"You must be Mr. Chase." Dr Winter wiped the soil from his palms onto his tweed jacket and outstretched it to Oliver. His emerald eyes were kind as he took in his new pupil.

"Yes, this is Oliver, Dr. Winter." A sugary sweet voice pierced my ears from my left as Reema waltzed up to us wearing a tiny sundress. Her long brown legs shimmered like gold beneath the sunlight poking through the greenhouse glass. Did she not own *any* items of clothing that covered her perfect skin?

I suddenly hated my khaki pants.

Reema walked over to the other side of Oliver and placed a hand on his shoulder, and I tensed as he casually let go of my hand. It was probably just a coincidence, but also annoying.

"It's nice to meet you, sir." Oliver shook the old Fae's hand, his face lighting up with nervous excitement. The face that I couldn't get enough of.

"Please, call me Donald." Dr. Winter strolled around the planter and started to make his way down one of the stone paths. "Come," was all he said over his shoulder and the three of us rushed after him, trudging further into the flora and fauna of the greenhouse.

Vines stretched out to us, forcing us to brush them away as some of them grew a little too aggressive, gripping our arms and ankles as we passed.

"Sorry about the Elder Vines. They hardly ever see any new faces in the greenhouse. Curious little devils." Dr. Winter smiled at our trio when we reached the opposite end of the greenhouse where another small table was set up with pots of dirt and a bowl of water.

Dr. Winter motioned for Oliver to join him on one side of the table and Reema and I stood on the other. "Now. I hear that you might be wielding some elemental magic. Can you tell me exactly what you have experienced?" The professor took out a small pad of paper and pen, eagerly awaiting Oliver's story.

Oliver relayed all that had happened since he was a child when he would get angry or, even, elated with the winds and fire. He left out the part about his father, but with all the other details, I'm sure he felt it was an unnecessary piece of personal information.

"And that's when Calina told me what she thought was happening. Which, of course, I thought was crazy. Because...it's crazy...right?" He stumbled on his words. "But then she brought me here. And now. Now I think I've either been blind my entire life, or I've actually lost my mind."

The old Fae nodded to his pad then placed his pen in his shirt pocket. "I see. Well, I can tell you that you certainly haven't lost your mind. This is all very real. And it sounds like you, indeed, have some untapped special abilities." Dr. Winter pulled the bowl of water closer to Oliver. "If it's ok, I'd like to try a couple of simple spells. To see if you can truly call upon the elements. And, if so, which ones. Most Fae can only control one or two. And witches may only gain control of one with years of honing their skill. Only Elementals can wield all four, and that is extremely rare, indeed."

Oliver looked at me, and I gave him a small nod. He then gave his adorable half smile to the professor.

"First things first. Relax. Place both hands on the bowl in front of you." Dr. Winter waited for Oliver to follow his command. "Now. Close your eyes. I want you to focus on something that makes you smile. Makes you excited."

Oliver peeked his eyes open and winked at me before closing them again. Heat rushed through my body and the color crept up my neck and face. I glanced at Reema, who had her arms crossed tightly over her chest, clearly annoyed.

"Concentrate on the feeling, Mr. Chase. Breathe. In. And out."

Oliver stood still as a statue, with his hands on the sides of the bowl, for several minutes and nothing happened. Dr. Winter jerked his chin to me, silently asking me to come over to them. I obeyed and the professor said, "Place your hands over Mr. Chase's, Miss Strovsky. Keep your concentration, son."

I inched close to Oliver and rested my chest against his back. Tentatively, I wrapped my arms around him, gently placing them over his, heat emanating from both of our bodies. I laid my hands over his and let my fingers intertwine with his. I heard his heartbeat faster and I whispered into his ear, reminding him to calm himself. His back muscles tensed underneath my embrace and his breathing slowed again.

"That's it! Maintain your focus," the Professor exclaimed.

I peeked over Oliver's shoulder, hearing the excitement in Dr. Winter's voice. The water in the bowl rippled slightly. Then tiny waves formed and crested over the surface of the water in the bowl.

"Oliver. Look," I said quietly into his ear. His cheeks flushed at the caress of my voice in his ear. He opened his eyes and his breath caught as he stared in shock at the miniature ocean that he had created. I released him from my hold and stepped back around the table to stand next to Reema.

"Very good, Mr. Chase." Dr. Winter reached for the pot filled with soil. "Now let's see what you can do when upset. And with another element." He put the pot in front of Oliver as he did with the water bowl. "This should be easier. It is an unfortunate thing, but magic is at its best through extreme anger or duress. Thus, those that can wield it, *especially* Elementals, need to practice caution and learn control."

Oliver's jaw clenched, his brown eyes a shade darker, and he slightly nodded.

"Same idea here. Place your hands on the pot but think of something that is upsetting. And it is ok to allow your anxieties to creep in this time."

Oliver listened to his teacher and closed his hands around the pot with his eyes shut. Unlike the first exercise, it didn't take any longer than a second for something to happen.

A tiny green sprout poked out of the soil in the pot. It slowly grew taller and budded a delicate white rose surrounded by thick golden thorns. It was beautiful. I had a hard time accepting that it was created using negative thoughts as energy.

The four of us looked on, breathless, as the unique rose plant continued to grow and grow until it was almost six feet in height. The vine then shot up with an alarming speed, bursting through the glass ceiling above and sending a rain of glass down towards the ground.

The sound of the growing vine and broken glass was deafening, and Oliver immediately stopped whatever he had done, and we all ducked under the table for cover. Dr. Winter stretched out an arm to the monstrous plant that now towered over a hundred feet above the greenhouse. His face was beet red and scrunched together in concentration. The plant finally stopped growing and slowly retreated back down to earth and disappeared beneath the soil where it had come from.

It was eerily silent except for the sound of all of our panting. Dr. Winter edged back to the table where the pot of soil stood innocently as if it didn't just birth a freakishly giant plant.Oliver's face had lost all color and I couldn't tell if it was fear or sadness on his face. Maybe it was despair. I went to grab his hand and Reema beat me to it, taking his hand in hers, patting it like he was a child who needed comforting.

He looked like he was in shock and let Reema lead him out from under the table with Dr. Winter. I tried to shake off my growing irritation as I watched her comfort him and stepped out into the open, broken glass crunching under my shoes as I went.

The color was slowly returning to Oliver's face, and he gently drew his hand away from Reema's. That's when I noticed the trembling. Something in me broke as it had when he told me about his father. He turned toward me, and I tried to smile to convey that it was all going to be ok.

"Impressive. And if what you said is true about fire and wind, well..." Dr. Winter was actually smiling, even with the damage done to the roof of the greenhouse.

"Excuse me?" Oliver looked at the teacher as if he had two heads. He threw his hands up, gesturing to the destruction. "I just busted your roof. We almost got impaled!"

"Yes." Dr. Winter nodded and grinned at Oliver. "There is much we need to practice. But don't you see? You are, indeed, an Elemental. It's been almost thirty years since I've seen one." He narrowed his eyes. "You look just like her."

Oliver's hands were still trembling from his green thumb mishap, and he crossed his arms over his chest when he noticed I was looking. His attention turned to Dr. Winter. "What do you mean I look like her? Who do I look like?"

"Your mother, I would gander."

Oliver shook his head, and he paced around the table. "No. My mother isn't magical, or an Elemental, or...whatever." He continued his pacing, now wringing his hands together.

"I would never forget an Elemental. Especially one as powerful as Ida." Dr. Winter had a faraway gleam in his eyes as if he were remembering the best of days past. "And, come to think of it, her husband, John, was even more so." He shook his head, lost in his memories, "That kind of power...together, they could have changed the world. Or ruled it."

Oliver stopped pacing. "Ida is my mom's name, but it has to be just a coincidence. She has only been married once. To my father, Edward Chase." He walked toward me and took my hand in his. "I think you're mistaking my mom for someone else. Thank you. For trying." Oliver backed away, taking me with him. "C'mon, Cali."

Dr. Winter studied Oliver for a moment like he was debating with himself over something, then simply nodded and folded his hands in front of him. "Perhaps. Well, Mr. Chase, this has been fascinating and I hope to see you again soon."

I gave Oliver's hand a little squeeze. Reema and I both extended our own gratitude to Dr. Winter, and I let Oliver guide the way out of the greenhouse.

Chapter 13

Oliver didn't say much as we left the greenhouse, and I didn't press him. I honestly couldn't imagine what it must have been like to be inundated with all of this unbelievable information. And in such a short time span. Just last month, he was a normal human who played guitar and had no idea what he wanted to be when he grew up.

And now, he was an Elemental.

A powerful one, it seemed. And so was his mother. That was a fact that I absolutely did not want to bring up with Oliver. Not yet anyway.

Reema walked with us back to my car, much too close to Oliver for my comfort, but he didn't seem to even notice she was still there.

"Are we still on for tomorrow morning?" Reema's syrupy voice drawled as she flashed him an overly seductive smile.

Gross. I cringed internally. It was obvious that he was into me, but I still couldn't bury the urge to vomit when Reema attempted to flirt with him.

Oliver had his hands in his pockets and stared at the ground. He raised his eyebrows slightly as if he just realized she had asked him something. "Hmm? Oh. Yeah, tomorrow is still good." His mouth curved into a tight-lipped smile before he returned his focus to the ground.

I held up my hand and waved my fingers at her. "Bye."

She lightly touched Oliver's shoulder. "See you tomorrow." Then Reema rolled her eyes at me and sauntered off.

I went to get into the car but paused, noticing Oliver leaning on the hood, lost in thought. I stuffed the keys into my pocket and stood next to him, close enough that our shoulders touched. I waited for him to say something. Anything. But he remained silent.

I gently nudged him. "Hey." I faced him and he turned toward me.

"Hey."

"It's been a long day." I cautiously twisted my fingers around his and looked up at the rising full moon. "Want to see something kind of cool?" I held those beautiful brown eyes with mine. "It's a little crazy..."

Oliver finally smiled, a genuine smile that lit up his face, and he let out a laugh. "Haven't I hit my quota for 'crazy' already?"

◭ ◭ ◭ ◭

I had never brought a boy home to meet my dad before. In fact, I had never brought *anyone* home before, other than Shani. And this wasn't just a normal "meeting the parents" situation. It was meeting the Erlking. Behind the veil.

We waited until the sun had completely set and I led Oliver down into the valley once more, but instead of going towards the Academy, we ventured deeper in the opposite direction. Almost as if we were headed back to Freyshire.

"Are we going back into town?" Oliver held my hand as we trudged over the trails on foot, the pitch of night making the stroll treacherous. "We could have driven," Oliver murmured as he tripped over a root sticking out of the ground.

I didn't exactly tell him where we were going.

I mean, he probably wouldn't have wanted to go. So.

"We can't drive to where we are going. And we are almost there." I pulled him along through the darkness before coming to an abrupt stop. The air had changed from the usual damp and dense feeling of the valley to a crisp and eerie stillness. The blackness of night faded, and an ethereal blue haze surrounded us as we approached a small wooden bridge that was seemingly in the middle of nowhere. Leading to nowhere.

"Why do I feel like I'm suddenly in a horror movie?" Oliver looked at the bridge and the emptiness that swirled around us. He gripped my hand, pulling me to a stop and I could practically smell the blood racing through his vessels. "Where are we?"

"Calm down. It looks a lot scarier than it is." I motioned towards the end of the bridge with my head. "This is the way...home. To my dad's house, anyway." I shrugged. "Surprise?"

"You are taking me to your dad's house." It was more of a statement than a question. "No, this is actually way scarier than it looks. Didn't you say that your dad was the Erlking? He's like a demon, right? The one that is famous for stealing and eating children?"

"Please, that was only one time!"

Oliver's mouth hung open in raw terror.

I rolled my eyes and laughed. "I'm kidding. He's not a demon. He's technically a Faerie, and not one who eats children. Come on. He's not that terrifying. Even for the Faery of Death."

"The...*what?*"

"Nothing. Come on!" I led Oliver over the wooden bridge to seemingly nothingness, but as we reached the end of the bridge, a heavy fog enveloped us as we crossed behind the veil. The crisp air grew humid and heavy, giving off a putrid smell that even I had a tough time stomaching as we moved into another realm.

The cool air returned, and the fog lifted. Oliver and I were almost gagging as we stood on the drive that led to the ancient castle that my dad called home. Black and green mildew coated the gray bricks that covered the exterior and three magnificent spires shot up toward the night sky. Moss and vines crawled around each spire and the windows of the castle. Though the town just beyond the veil was experiencing mild temperatures and clear skies, the air by my dad's place was frigid and snowflakes swirled around us.

"Wow."

"Right? This is home." Pride surged through me as I held my arms out ceremoniously presenting the old castle like a prize to behold. "You are officially behind the veil."

"You come here every month?"

I nodded and jerked my chin up to the full moon hanging low amidst a sea of cloud cover. "The bridge we crossed to get here is only visible to creatures on full moons, and that's the only time they can cross it to come behind the veil. But, even then, one has to be invited. And my invitation is always open." I smiled and took his hand. "Come on. Let's go meet my dad."

We walked down the drive and opened the two massive wooden doors. Oliver was a bit shell-shocked at the sight of the interior with its velvet red curtains, opulently decorated rooms, and ornate light fixtures. "This is incredible. It's like we've traveled back to the medieval times or something."

"Yes, that is when I acquired this palace. I believe it was in the year of 1321, in fact."

My soul nearly left my body at the sound of my father's voice behind us. I jerked around to see him standing in the foyer. He wore his typical sleek black jacket and burgundy vest, and his long black hair was tied neatly behind his head. His hands were neatly folded behind his back; he was immaculate and statue-like as he sized up my guest.

"Calina. Are you going to introduce me to your...friend?" His pale, nearly translucent face was unreadable. I hated when he acted so cold.

"I'm Oliver. It's a pleasure to meet you, Sir." Oliver swallowed hard and he held out his hand to my father.

My dad stared at Oliver's hand for a moment, and I widened my eyes at him, hoping to relay how important it was that he *not* embarrass me. He narrowed his eyes at me then, what felt like a lifetime later, shook Oliver's hand.

"A pleasure." The Erlking's grip was a bit tight, and Oliver winced slightly before my dad released his grip. "I am Calina's father. Welcome to my home." My father glared at me. "I trust you and your guest will stay in the East Wing?" It was an order, even though it sounded like a question.

"Of course."

He nodded. "I will see you both at dinner. Six o'clock. Sharp." He turned toward the West Wing and then spoke over his shoulder. "It is nice to meet you, Oliver." With that he vanished.

"What's in the West Wing?" Oliver had a wicked grin as if his only thought was to break the one rule of the house.

"My dad's servants...and hunting party."

Oliver raised an eyebrow suggestively.

I simply shook my head and chuckled. "No, we can't go snooping. Magic or no magic, living beings can't enter."

"Bummer."

"We can tour the other side of the castle, though. Want to see upstairs?"

I showed Oliver all of the hidden stairwells and secret passages, slowly making our way to my own tower. I led him up the narrow spiral staircase to my room. Only to show him the view. That was it.

I mean, it did have the best view in the castle.

A nervous energy rushed through me as we crossed the threshold into my bedroom, and I attempted to swallow down my anxiety.

"This is cozy." Oliver still held my hand as he scanned my bedroom, most likely judging my twin teddy bears sitting near my pillows. And the unicorn poster on my closet door. Damn, I really needed to update my space.

I cringed.

Then panicked remembering the window and what the best view was as he stepped over to the floor to ceiling window and stared out.

I prayed he wouldn't notice how clearly you could see his cottage, but his head cocked to the side, "Huh."

I brushed past the obvious. "Yeah, you can see all of Freyshire from here."

He turned to me, brow furrowed but still with a hint of a smile. "You sure can. In fact, there is a really great view of my house."

I walked over to stand next to him, peering out the window. "Hmm, I hadn't really noticed. I mean, I saw you the other night, but I thought it was a one off..." I felt his eyes on me. Studying me. I kept my eyes glued on the view of the town, attempting to maintain an innocent expression.

"I've only seen you a couple of times. Just how many times have you seen me?" He was still watching me, and I tried not to look at him, as a smile spread over my lips.

"Calina? Have you been stalking me?" He was beaming now, and he was trying not to laugh.

"Maybe. 'Casual' stalking." I attempted to keep a serious expression but we both erupted in laughter, and he slid his arm around my waist, pulling me closer.

His lips brushed against my ear, and he whispered, "You know I haven't actually *kissed* you yet." Chills ran down my spine and I closed my eyes, leaning into him. His lips remained mere millimeters away from my ear, then my cheek, and I turned my head slightly to face him.

His gaze traveled from my eyes to my lips and his thumb traced softly along the curves of my mouth. My lips parted slightly under his touch, impatiently awaiting the moment where his mouth would capture mine.

He lowered his left hand, gripping my waist tightly and his other hand caressed my cheek as he pressed his lips to mine. He kissed me gently at first and his tongue parted my lips, finding mine. Then, his kiss intensified. Need and passion flowed through him, and he pressed his body against me, sending heat and shockwaves down to the space between my legs.

Oliver didn't allow his hands to travel, seemingly elated in the kiss alone. It was a nice feeling, not needing or rushing into anything more. Just being in that moment.

It was nice. Torturous, but nice.

Both of his hands rested on my hips now and he gripped the ends of my shirt in his fists at my sides, pulling his hungry mouth away from my kiss. He rested his forehead to mine and met my gaze, his eyes a stunning amber color under the light of the full moon hovering so close to my window.

His breathing was ragged, and his heart raced in that addicting melody that threatened to make my bloodlust take over. I took a deep and steadying breath, biting my lip to keep from biting his, and eased out of his grip.

He leaned his shoulder against the window, watching me as I edged away from him. It was an effort to not run back into his arms. I steadied myself on my white dresser on the other side of the room and we stared at one another for a moment. The scent of him was overwhelming and I wrung my sweating palms together trying to focus on anything else.

Thankfully, my attention was pulled to the sky outside the window behind Oliver. Streaks of lightning danced in the sky, and thunder clapped loudly in the distance. The winds had picked up, blowing up small branches and debris in small funnels over the grounds around the castle.

Oliver noticed the shift in my gaze and turned to look out the window. His shoulders sank slightly, and he gripped the back of his neck. He said to the window, "I can learn to control it. Right?"

I ignored the bloodlust that had turned my throat into sandpaper, and I went over to stand next to him again. "Yes."

A simple answer but it seemed to suffice. He nodded and rested his forehead against the glass, silently watching the windstorm he had accidentally summoned.

I checked my watch. "We should go. It's dinnertime and pissing off my dad would be more dangerous than any magic you can conjure."

Chapter 14

Oliver and I somehow managed to survive through a meal with the Erlking and I took him back to his house around midnight.

I was glad to hear him talk nearly the whole walk then ride back into town. He seemed like he was finally in a better headspace, and I had a smile on my face listening to him talk animatedly about the book he was currently reading and his upcoming lacrosse game.

We slowed as we came up the cobblestone path that led to his small brick cottage on the edge of town. Oliver had grown quiet, and we both lingered along the path in front of his door. He had his hands buried in his pockets and stared up at the moon.

"Thank you for taking me behind the veil. Your dad seemed...nice."

I laughed. "Sure. Nice."

"Okay, he was pretty scary. But I think he liked me." Oliver smiled.

"I'm sure he did."

He sighed and shook his head as he gazed at the bright rock in the sky. "I still can't believe it's real. I still can't believe any of what I've seen recently is real." He looked back at me now but kept his hands where they were. I wondered if he was afraid to touch me in case it caused more elemental disasters. "And you were right. It was crazy. But I think that might be a new normal for me."

"Most likely." I inched toward him, and he subtly took a step back. "Are you ok?"

The muscle in his cheek tensed and he appeared just as nervous as the first time we met. He shrugged but didn't say anything.

"I know there has been a lot to. To process." I attempted another cautious step forward. "We will get you more training with Dr. Winter. And, as for what he said about your mom..."

Anger flashed in Oliver's eyes, and I let my thoughts die in the midnight air. I reached for his hand and pulled him to me. I took his face in my hands. "I promise. We will figure it all out."

He narrowed his eyes at me for a moment, studying my face and reading my expression. "Are you trying to vamp me right now?"

I burst out laughing, dropping my hands from his cheeks. "'Vamp' you?"

A chuckle escaped him too. "You know, using that compulsion thing on me? Controlling me?" Oliver wrapped his arms around my waist and pulled my body to his. "Making me want to be near you all the time?" His forehead rested against mine, and one of his hands moved to my cheek where his fingertips grazed against my skin. "Causing me to ignore the insanity that has become my life just to make sure you keep wanting to hang out with me?" The laughter was gone from his eyes as he stared at me intently, then whispered, "There has to be a reason why you have such a hold over me."

I held my breath, fiery heat blazing throughout my entire body. I couldn't look away from those amber eyes. "I'm just that amazing," I said sarcastically but a bit breathless. My lips curved into a slight smirk, trying to cut the mounting sexual tension.

"Yes, you are," he said and brushed his lips against mine, softly. Barely there. He eased back slightly, and I leaned into him, pressing my lips back to his, basking in the warmth of his arms and chest against me, all around me.

He gently pulled his mouth from mine and held me close into his chest, resting his cheek against my head. His embrace was filled with longing, and I knew he was scared to go too far, not knowing how his power might react.

Again, pure torture.

We stayed locked in that embrace for several moments before I noticed the cobblestone path under our feet. "Oliver, look." We both looked down and smiled at dozens of beautiful tulip blossoms of orange and pink and red sprouting up all around us, lining the pathway from the front steps of his house down to the end of the street.

▲▲▲▲

I replayed our kiss in my mind the entire night and through most of my classes the next morning. Mostly to distract myself from the knowledge that Oliver was with Reema until two that afternoon.

I closed my eyes, imagining his arms around me, one of his songs playing in the background of my daydream, when I felt a warm hand on my shoulder.

"Miss Strovsky."

Ms. Dunning was standing next to me. The rest of the classroom was empty. I must have missed the dismissal. How long had I been daydreaming? "I'm sorry—"

"Miss Strovsky, you missed our tutoring session last week."

Shit. I knew I was forgetting something. I had been so focused on Oliver, I had completely forgotten about tutoring. I honestly couldn't remember being in any of my classes over the past couple weeks. It was like my body was on auto-drive, taking me to places without bringing my mind.

"Ms. Dunning, I can explain, I—"

"Yes, I know what you have been doing." Ms. Dunning did not look impressed. She slowly walked up to the front of the room and began erasing the white board.

I reluctantly followed. "How? Are you able to read my thoughts?" That wasn't a vampire power, typically, but I had been surprised at others' talents before.

She continued to wipe the board, her lithe limbs barely putting in an effort. "Please, Calina, I am not a demigod." She turned to face me. "I spoke with Dr. Winter. He told me about your friend. Dr. Winter sounded quite excited about your friend's talents."

"His name is Oliver. And he might be an Elemental. He's—"

She shook her head. "Calina, I am concerned about you."

"I know I missed tutoring, and I am near failing your course, but I promise I can pull my grade up." I pointed a finger to the ceiling and added excitedly, "And I will meet with you more than once a week if I need to!"

Ms. Dunning held her slender hand up, stomping on my resolve to do better at being a vampire. "That is not why I am worried. From what Dr. Winter has told me, Oliver might be related to some powerful Elementals. These creatures are dangerous, Miss Strovsky. I urge you to use caution." Fear shone in her glacier blue eyes. "Some things are meant to stay hidden."

▲ ▲ ▲ ▲

I was stuck in my own head for the rest of the day, Ms. Dunning's warning replaying itself like a broken record. Did she know Oliver's mother? It sure sounded like she was terrified of whomever Oliver inherited his magic from. It was just one more piece in the puzzle that didn't fit. Dr. Winter was excited about Oliver's magic. And his mom, for that matter. If the woman in question *was* Oliver's mom.

"Cali?" Shani was looking at me with her brow furrowed. Had she asked me something?

"I'm sorry. I was—"

"Thinking of Oliver. I know. Please don't imagine him naked in front of me, ok?" She shook her head and shuddered.

"It wouldn't be a big deal if you would keep out of my thoughts." I quickly pictured Oliver and his perfect smile. I wasn't ready to talk about Ms. Dunning's advice to steer clear.

She sighed. "Whatever. Can we please get back to this whole lacrosse game thing?"

I looked at her questioningly and she sighed, frustrated.

"The lacrosse game? Against Freyshire College?" She sounded exasperated. "Oh my gods, you heard absolutely nothing I've said. Oliver's college is playing St. Anne's in two weeks...he asked us to go? Anyway, I think I want to go to the game and maybe invite the cocktail server from Bloody Goode's. But I don't want to unless you're going."

"Yeah, sure," I said noncommittedly. "Maybe I can get him another meeting with Dr. Winter this week sometime."

Shani perked up. "Has Oliver asked his mom about his magic yet?"

"No. I haven't pressed him about it either. I think he is still in denial that she would keep such an important secret from him."

"I guess that makes sense. I can't imagine how he must be feeling."

I couldn't either. But I didn't say as much.

Shani stood and grabbed her bookbag by the front door. "You should go see your mom. Maybe she knew Oliver's mom from the Academy...if his mom is actually a creature." She gave me a quick hug and picked up her phone on the kitchen counter. "I've got to get to my Macro class. Remember to tell Oliver about the game, ok?" She smiled and walked out of the dorm.

I nodded. I would tell him about the game. And also, ask to meet his mom. Creatures could sense other creatures, and if she recognized me as a vampire, then she was definitely what I suspected.

Shani had had a good idea too, though. My mom may have met or known something about powerful Elementals when she went to school here. Dr. Winter said that Elementals were rare, so most likely they would have been a hot topic of gossip back in the day.

I glanced at the clock on the wall over the microwave. One forty-five. She would just be getting ready for work. I could swing by and catch her before she left.

My mom was an exotic dancer. And I knew how that sounded but honestly, she was incredibly gorgeous, being a vampire and all. Plus, it was a great job that she could keep long term without anyone noticing she didn't exactly age. There was so much turnover at the club, no one knew who was in charge on any given day, and the clientele were usually drunk. So.

My mother had full custody of me after my parent's divorce, outside of the full-moon visits with dad. And, of course, holidays. And, even though we had lived in her tiny cottage on the edge of town ever since before I could remember, every time I saw it, it was as if I was seeing it for the first time.

It was the only cottage in the neighborhood, maybe even in the whole town, that wasn't brown brick and wood timber. Oh no, my mother couldn't stand being normal or plain and "like everyone else". Her house was covered in a deep red wooden siding, with black shutters that lined the oversized windows. The front door was lit by a bronzed chandelier so large that it nearly brushed the top of my head, and the porch was decorated with an outdoor sofa that had red cushions and two black rocking chairs that looked like they were taken straight from the 1700's.

They probably were.

It was shocking to me that no one had ever suspected that my mother was a vampire. Or a witch. Or something else completely terrifying. If I was a human and had no idea that creatures were living in the same town as I was, I would have been fearful of my mom's place. Or at least turned off by its utter tackiness.

When I approached the front door, I ducked under the dangling black crystal tail of the chandelier and let myself in. As per usual, all of the lights were off except for a single lamp with a red cloth draped over its shade, giving off the appearance of the red-light district.

Or so I've heard.

"Mom? Are you here?" I called for her from the door, afraid I might see something that I couldn't erase from memory. I heard shuffling and mumbling from her bedroom on the far side of the living room and waited for her to emerge.

"Hi, honey!" My mother strolled out into the living room, wearing a red strappy mini dress that might have been lingerie, and walked straight over to me, enveloping me in her frigid embrace. She smelled like an odd mixture of jasmine and cocoa butter, but the scent reminded me of my childhood. I held her tightly and breathed her in, not realizing just how much I had missed her since I left for the Academy even though we spoke on the phone almost daily.

I reluctantly pulled away from the safety of her arms and we took a seat on the black leather sofa.

"I feel like it's been ages since I've seen you. You hardly drop by anymore, and you spend every weekend with *him*." My mom wouldn't even say the word "dad", let alone speak his name. It was like he was Voldemort or something.

"It's not even been three months, mom, and I only go to *dad's* once a month. Like I have since birth. Plus, I stop by here all the time when I'm in town."

My mom sat back slightly, giving me the once over. "It's not the same. But never mind all that. Tell me everything. Is St. Anne's everything you hoped it would be?" She didn't give me a chance to respond. "I remember how much I loved it there. The classes, the valley magic...the guys." She smiled wickedly and patted my knee. "So, is there a guy? Two?"

"Mom! No, I mean, yes. There is a guy. One guy."

"Ok, not exactly like my own experience at St. Anne's, but one guy is great. So, tell me about him. Is he another vampire? Ooh, or maybe one of those sexy tree nymphs?" She had a far off look in her eyes. "Mmhmm, those nymphs really have some unexpected stamina. And talk about flexible. If I was about 200 years younger…"

Gross. "Mom, you're a vampire. Age isn't something that you should worry about."

She shrugged. "You know what I mean."

"I guess." I shuddered, trying to erase the unwanted images of my mom sleeping her way through college.

"I'm sorry. Tell me about your new man." She clapped her hands excitedly, her long red fingernails tapping each other with every beat.

"His name is Oliver. And he doesn't go to St. Anne's." Ugh. My mother was not going to like this. "He's a…human. Sort of." I mumbled the last part under my breath.

"He's a human, 'sort of'?" My mother dropped her excited hands into her lap and her icy stare bore into me.

"Yes, but—"

She held her hand up to stop my explanation. I waited for her to start screaming and racing about the living room on some hysterical rant about creatures and how humans ruin everything, blah, blah. But she stayed silent and continued to stare me down, making me want to dissolve into the couch cushion.

"Oh, hey, Calina." My mom's *human* boy-toy strolled in from the bedroom wearing nothing but a towel around his hips.

"Hi, Derek." I watched as Derek padded into the kitchen and grabbed an apple before retreating back into the bedroom. I couldn't help but notice the two bite marks on his neck. And chest. And...well, only one was peeking out from the towel.

I rolled my eyes and turned back to my mom who was still glowering at me. Did the woman ever blink? "I think it's pretty ridiculous that you can sit here and look all pissed off at me about Oliver when you have Derek over every night."

Her expression finally softened, and she shifted her gaze, examining her nails. "You know very well that Derek is nothing more to me than a plaything. He is under strict compulsion and has no idea who or what we are. And there's a good reason for that."

"I know. And I get that. But Oliver isn't a typical human. In fact, he might not even be a human at all. He's got some abilities that I've never seen...he might be an Elemental."

My mom stopped looking at her nailbeds and focused on me again. "What do you mean, 'might be'? That's a rare creature, and if you said he was a human, does that mean he has been keeping it a secret? Or didn't know?"

"All of the above?" I told my mom all about how Oliver could see me through the veil, the strange elemental incidents that happened around him, and our trip to the Academy to work with Dr. Winter. "Dr. Winter said something about a student named Ida. He assumed that she was Oliver's mother."

My mom's brow furrowed as she tried to recall an Ida from her memory bank. "I remember an Ida. She was a year ahead of me and I didn't know her very well, but I do remember her being a Teaching Assistant in my Elemental Magic course." She glanced behind her to the bedroom to make sure we weren't being listened to. "Ida was powerful. I had never seen anything like her before and haven't since. Except my Professor. I think they may have been dating, come to think of it."

I nodded. "That's what Dr. Winter said. He told us that Ida married the Professor, and that's why Oliver insists it's a different Ida and not his mother. His father wasn't a teacher."

"Elementals aren't born to humans either." She raised an eyebrow suggestively and I knew exactly what she was saying.

"Do you think that Oliver's father may have been the Professor? Just changed his name for some reason?" I answered my own question before she had a chance. "No, that just doesn't add up. Maybe Ida from the Academy is a different woman."

She shrugged. "I don't know, but listen, if your boy is somehow mixed up with my old Elementals Professor, you need to stay away. That man is dangerous."

Ms. Dunning heeded the same warning. Who was this guy? I opened my mouth to ask the hundreds of new questions that suddenly invaded my brain, but I was interrupted when Derek came back out of the bedroom, fully dressed this time.

He took a seat next to my mother and I stood. "Thanks, mom. I'll call you tomorrow."

She simply nodded, but her eyes told me so much more.

To be cautious. To keep anything that I found out about Oliver's parents to myself.

Chapter 15

I asked to meet Oliver at his house around seven that evening. I needed to see his mother. His sisters. Maybe they all shared the same powers as Oliver. Maybe none of them did and he was an enigma. Either way, I had to know. For his sake.

I rang the doorbell and impatiently waited for him to answer, pacing around the tiny front porch. Maybe this wasn't a good idea after all. It wasn't my business. Nor would it be my place to tell him. If there was anything to tell.

I stopped in my tracks as the door swung open.

"Hello. Can I help you?" a shorter woman who looked to be in her early fifties was standing behind the screen door, giving me a once over. Her graying hair was pulled into a messy ponytail that rested on her neck. She wore a floral top paired with khaki capris and a frilly pink apron layered with a fresh coat of flour.

"Yes, ma'am, I'm—"

Oliver now stood beside the woman and opened the screen door. "Hey." His perfect grin lit up his face. "Mom, this is Calina." He glanced at his mother then at me, still holding the door open. "Want to come in?"

His mother's eyes darkened, and she seemed apprehensive at the thought of me entering their home. But she moved aside as I stepped over the threshold.

I tried to read her expression, trying to gauge if she could tell what I was. It was nearly impossible for me to get a feel for who or what she truly was. It was as if she were using some kind of cloaking spell to cover up her identity.

Or she was a human. And I was nuts.

I scanned the sage green walls of the living room. It looked like a typical cottage with family photos lining the walls and a tan couch and matching ottoman situated in front of a television that was perched over a white brick fireplace. The living room opened up to a small dining area where a long wooden table was centered under a silver light fixture. Floral arrangements of roses and peonies in crystal blue vases were placed around both rooms, giving the home a sweet and homey aroma.

I searched my surroundings, feeling a little surprised at the normalcy of it all. I'm not sure what I expected. Black walls? Tied bundles of dried witch herbs hanging from the kitchen ceiling? I smirked to myself. If anything, Oliver's house was decorated in a stylish and modern motif.

But still there was something...off. Though the décor was exceptionally average, my stomach flipped, and a strange feeling weighed on me and seemed to flow throughout their entire tiny cottage.

What was she hiding in there?

I thrust my hand out to her. "It's nice to meet you, Ms. Chase." She had her arms crossed protectively over her chest and tentatively took my hand in hers, shaking it for a millisecond before placing her arms over herself once more. Her heartbeat quickened for the briefest moment, then relaxed just as quickly, as if she were actively attempting to slow her pulse.

She knew what I was. Or she could, at least, sense that I was a creature of some kind.

And she was scared. Of me.

Oliver had a strange expression on his face as he witnessed the exchange between me and his mother. He gave me a sidelong glance. "Uh, we are just going to get some dinner." He stood a whole head taller than his mother and had to lean down to give her a quick kiss on the cheek. "I won't be home too late."

"Ok, hon," His mother said, tilting her cheek up to Oliver but never taking her eyes from me.

Oliver turned to me. "Let me grab my wallet. I'll be right back." He looked nervously between the two of us again before exiting the room.

Leaving me alone. With her.

She stared me down. "I know what you are." She finally said after an eternity.

"Ms. Chase, I—" I started.

"I know what you are, and I want you to stay away from my son. I have spent the last twenty years protecting him from that world. It's not safe for him."

I opened my mouth to respond and closed it again as Oliver walked back into the foyer.

"Ready?"

I nodded and let him lead me out the front door without a second glance at his mother.

▲▲▲▲

"Sorry about my mom. I haven't introduced her to a girl before." Oliver laughed between bites of cheesecake at Mama's. "She's a bit overprotective, I guess. You know, 'only son' stuff."

I nodded and smiled along at the joke, but I couldn't stop thinking about what she had said about "protecting" him. From his identity? It made no sense. What was so dangerous about knowing who you were?

I mean, aside from the whole "discovering that you were a supernatural creature" thing.

"Are you ok? You seem a little distracted."

I refocused on my dessert and Oliver. "Yeah, I'm good. Actually, I meant to tell you that Shani and I are going to go to the lacrosse game against Freyshire College in a couple of weeks."

He appeared confused. "Are we playing St. Anne's?"

Right. I kept forgetting that anyone who wasn't raised with creature knowledge were magicked to never give the Academy a second thought. I simply nodded.

Oliver grinned. "That's awesome! But now I guess I will have to practice more so I don't completely embarrass myself in front of you."

I shrugged. "Impossible. Besides, I'm more interested to see what you notice about the players and spectators from St. Anne's. Now that you know…" I made sure no one was in earshot and leaned across the table with a wicked smile. "Now that you know who, or *what*, to look for."

"That sounds both intriguing and terrifying. Hopefully I won't get too distracted." Oliver smiled and shoved the last bite of his cheesecake into his mouth.

"You'll be fine. Shani wants to ask the server from Bloody Goode's to come, and she will probably bring Reema too."

He shifted in his seat some. "Fun." The comment was coated in sarcasm, and he shook his head. "Sorry. Reema is just. Well." He seemed to be searching for the right word. "Forward?"

I laughed, nearly spitting out the cake I was chewing. "Just a little. She likes you. And she likes knowing she could have anyone she wants, even if that someone is my boyfriend."

His eyebrow lifted and his lips twitched, ever so slightly.

I froze.

Did I say that out loud? I swallowed and waited for his reaction to the "b-word".

He shyly looked out the window and a half-smile dimpled his cheek. I prayed it was due to me defining the relationship and not the fact that Reema wanted him.

He glanced back at me, melting me with that smile. "I wouldn't be a very good boyfriend if I was that easily swayed."

I flushed.

Oliver stood from the booth and held his hand out to me. "C'mon, walk me home."

He started down the street that led to his house, and I reached out and took his hand, pulling him to a stop. He paced back toward me, a half-smile and raised eyebrow. "Have something else in mind?"

"It's just a bit early." I cocked my head to the side. "Want to come out to the Academy? See what it's like after dark?"

"I could be down for that."

▲▲▲▲

The ride down the valley was a completely different experience in the dark. The "elegant" creatures were all in for the night, and the nocturnal animals roamed the hills. Flocks of bats swirled around, their leathery wings beating against the car doors, Chupacabra's lurked in the treetops threatening to pounce on the car's roof, and those pesky hellhounds didn't care what time of day or night it was. They were still out in droves.

Oliver didn't seem to be bothered by any of the night monsters strolling about. He didn't seem to notice anything but me, in fact. When he wasn't leaning into me, softly kissing my shoulder and neck, he laced his fingers with mine, contentedly resting his head on the seatback with his eyes peacefully closed.

It was becoming increasingly impossible to focus on the road ahead. Especially, when his hands traveled along my thigh as he lightly kissed and nibbled my earlobe. And the wind gusts picking up and blowing against the vehicle made the drive about ten times harder.

Maybe that's why retreated to his side of the car with his eyes closed for small intervals in between moments of teasing me. He must have been trying to calm himself to prevent any natural disasters.

When we finally arrived at the campus, I was so hot and bothered that my hands were shaking. I put the car in park, and we sat there for a moment, neither one of us moving. Or breathing.

Suddenly, he turned to me, grabbed my waist, and in one swift motion, hoisted me onto his lap from where he sat in the passenger seat. His eyes pierced through me, and his eager lips found mine, ravenous, as if he had waited years to kiss me.

My legs tightened around him, and I thrusted my hips closer, until I could feel his manhood harden beneath me. His hands gripped hard into my waist then slowly slid up the hemline of my tank top, his fingertips lightly grazing against my sides, my stomach, and then just barely brushing over my pert nipples.

I gasped, but didn't break our kiss, breathing him in. His lips curved into a smile beneath my kiss, and he pushed his hips upward while his thumbs expertly moved my bra aside, massaging my breasts. I threw my head back and instinctively pushed myself harder into him, wanting to feel him. All of him.

My nails dug into his muscular shoulders as I pulled him into me, kissing along his jawline, his neck, his collarbone, needing to taste him. I paused over his neck, breathing hard as the allure of his beating carotid called to me. I went back to kissing his mouth to distract myself from the growing urge to bite him.

His breath quickened and he allowed his hands to slide up my thighs, fingers exploring and inching higher and higher under my skirt until they found the warmth between my legs.

I moaned, biting my lip as his fingers danced their way in and out and all along my center. I drew in a ragged breath and allowed my own hands to travel, clumsily undoing the buttons of his shirt, marveling at the tight chest and ab muscles that lie beneath. I struggled to get the button of his pants undone as my own pleasure threatened to overtake me at any second.

I tried to slow my climax and my entire body tightened around his playful fingers before I finally got his damned button undone. He tensed under my legs as I explored all of him with my hand. I leaned into him once more nestling my face into his shoulder and the aroma of blood filled my nose and desire swept over me.

The overwhelming feeling of ecstasy of being that intimate with Oliver mixed with the added bonus of blood lust...it was...too much.

His touch.

The feel of his full length in my grasp.

The scent of his rushing blood.

I fought the urge for several moments, attempting to focus on how amazing Oliver made me feel and how much I wanted to take our make-out session to the next level. But then I heard his breath catch and he groaned against my ear.

The sound of his own gratification blended with the rhythmic pulsing of his blood sent me over the edge.

My own ending came simultaneously as my fangs pierced through the sensitive skin between his shoulder and neck and the sweet flow of his warm blood filled me with euphoria. The world stopped spinning. The only thing that was real was this moment. Ultimate pleasure blended with the rich, smoothness of a craving that I despised and loved all at once.

Oliver must have felt his release too, and I could feel his body tighten, pulling me closer as his heart rate quickened then began to beat slower and somewhat irregularly. He let a low growl escape against my ear and kissed me lightly on the neck.

But I couldn't stop indulging myself.

His grip on my hips felt a touch weaker, and he shifted slightly beneath me, but I held him closer, pulling deeper from the wound I created on his neck.

"Cali..." His hands pushed lightly against my waist. "Cali, stop."

I could feel him trying to pull away from my bite. Could feel the fear that was building up inside him. Could taste it, even. I knew I had to stop.

But I couldn't.

"Cali...please," Oliver whispered, and his hands were on my shoulders trying to push me off of him. "Stop. You have to...stop."

Stop. Stop!

His body went limp beneath mine and I forced myself away from him as fast as I could, practically jumping into the driver's seat putting as much distance between us as possible. Tears gathered at the brims of my eyes as I stared at Oliver slumped over in the passenger seat.

I waited for a second, but he didn't move. "Oliver?" Nothing.

Shit. *Shit!* A warm drip of blood rolled down the side of my chin and I swiped at it with the back of my hand. I silently cursed myself for allowing things to go as far as they did. What if he...no. I couldn't think like that. He definitely lost a lot of blood, but he was still alive. Right?

Oh my gods, I killed my boyfriend.

I shook myself out of my negative thought spiral. I watched him for another moment, noting a slight, but still present, rise and fall of his chest. He was breathing, but barely. I had to do something. Get him some help.

Immediately, I pressed against the door handle to get out of the car so I could pull him out and get him to the infirmary. But the door wouldn't budge. Something was blocking me from opening the door from the outside. Scratch that. Something was *covering* the door. Enveloping the entire car. I rolled down the window and tentatively pressed my hand on the thick green vines that had stretched and grown until they had swallowed the vehicle.

I had wondered, briefly, why no elemental incidents had occurred in the throes of our passion, but I guess they had.

This wasn't good.

I tried to summon my vampire strength and pushed my entire body against the door, but it was no use. We were stuck. I bit hard on my lip, panic setting in. How in the heck was I going to get Oliver out of there?

I peeked over at him again and he appeared to be stirring a bit. I exhaled in relief. Okay, one crisis averted. Now to see about the crazy vines that locked us in. I pushed against the door again, somehow thinking that maybe I grew stronger in the last two minutes.

"What are you doing?" Oliver's voice was quiet and hoarse.

I stopped trying to force the car door open and turned to face him. "How are you feeling?" I bit the inside of my cheek, nervous that he might freak out after...well, after I almost killed him.

"What happened?" Oliver rubbed his eyes with his palms and his brow furrowed as he tried to focus. He looked down at his unbuttoned pants, then over at me, the confusion replaced with a sexy smile as if he had just remembered what naughty things we had just done together.

I gulped and waited for him to fully remember.

His hand slowly moved to his neck then he assessed the blood smeared on his fingertips from where I had let my blood lust get the better of me. His gaze settled on me again. "You bit me." It wasn't a question. But it didn't sound like he was surprised or angry either.

"I'm so sorry. I couldn't...we were...it felt so amazing." I stumbled over my words, not knowing how to explain why I couldn't stop. Why I couldn't control myself. I stared at my hands. "I'm sorry."

He reached for my hand, and I pulled away. "Calina, it's ok."

I shook my head. "I could have killed you. This is too dangerous. Me and you...we can't."

"That's ridiculous, and you know it." He reached for my hand again and I let him take it this time. "Besides, I'm not sure if it's normal, but it kind of felt...good. The biting. Not the whole passing out thing." Color rushed to his face and his dimple appeared on his cheek.

Gods he was adorable.

He moved toward me and placed his hand on my cheek, forcing me to look into those beautiful eyes. "I'm not going anywhere. Dangerous or not." He tilted my chin and kissed me gently. He shrugged, "I mean, you're not the only one who can wreak havoc, you know."

I winced. "Right. About that." I tilted my head to the open window on the driver's side. "We may have a hard time getting out."

Chapter 16

A smile was plastered on my face for the rest of the week. I mean, sure it was kind of a pain to have to call Shani to come break us out of the vine jail but being with Oliver that night? Kissing him. Touching. I shivered as I recalled his hands all over me. And he was mine.

Boyfriend.

Oliver was perfect. He was beautiful and smart. And *my* boyfriend.

He was the only thing that had been on my mind. Which didn't do much good for my mid-term grades. I stopped briefly from applying mascara, thinking about the repercussions of being as distracted as I was.

Ugh, my dad was going to kill me. But, honestly, isn't dating and 'learning more about myself' the main purpose of freshman year? I shrugged at my own reflection and continued to apply my make-up. I was going to meet Oliver in an hour for a lesson with Dr. Winter, and I figured a little make-up couldn't hurt. I decided to try out some of Shani's plum lipstick and puckered my lips in the mirror as I primped and pulled invisible pieces of lint from my top.

"Your dad is definitely going to kill you." Shani responded to my thoughts from her bed. She had her nose buried in her Mythology book. She slammed it shut and looked at me through the mirror. "So is mine." Her nose crinkled in disgust. "I never realized just how messed up my family is. Do you know how many worlds were created and wars were started based on jealous gods and their sex organs?"

I just laughed and surveyed myself in the mirror. I opted for a sky-blue cowl-neck sweater that exposed one of my shoulders over black leggings and let my hair hang loose, the layers flowing like waves down my back. I wasn't sure why I was nervous. It was as if the new title of girlfriend had added some sort of extra pressure.

"Nothing has changed. If anything, it just means he's falling even harder for you."

Usually, I would have scolded Shani for reading my thoughts, but I kind of needed her pep talk. I smiled at her. "Thanks."

A knock at our dorm room door broke up our love fest.

"Are you expecting someone?" I wandered out of my room and headed towards the front door and Shani yelled, "No, it's probably Chuck 'checking in' on Reema again!"

I smiled to myself and swung open the door expecting to see our nosey RA. My smile instantly faded as soon as I was met with the suspicious eyes of Oliver's mother.

I took a step back and cocked my head to the side. "Ms. Chase. How? What. What are you doing here?"

She watched me for a moment then glanced down the hallway from where she came up from the stairwell. Almost as if she were making sure that no one had seen her. She leaned in slightly, "Can I come in?"

"Uh...yes. Of course." I backed into the dorm and let her slip in. She tugged her long black coat tighter around herself and crossed her arms over her chest.

"Who is it?" Shani's voice rang from the bedroom, and she sauntered out to where I was awkwardly standing next to Ms. Chase. She stopped short when she saw her. "Oh. Shit." Her hand flew to her mouth. "I'm sorry! I wasn't expecting—"

Ms. Chase put her hand up. "It's fine." She focused on me. "I need to talk to you." She looked back at Shani. "In private."

"Right. I'm going to go...anywhere but here." Shani widened her eyes at me then disappeared into the bedroom on the other side of the dorm.

"Please, sit down." I motioned to the couch. "Would you like something to drink?"

Ms. Chase shook her head. "No, thank you. I will be quick. When you came to the house, I told you that I know what you are."

I nodded.

"I'm an Elemental. But I think you may have figured that out. Now that you've seen what Oliver is...is capable of."

An excited energy washed over me. Maybe she was finally ok with letting Oliver be his true self. "He's powerful. And he wants to learn how to control it. Dr. Winter said he will help him. Train him to—"

"Dr. Winter?" She shook her head and held her hand up. "No." The edge in her voice caught me off guard. "Oliver can never come here. Not as a student. Honestly, he shouldn't come here at all. But he seems to be quite taken with you." She sized me up. "I just came here to tell you to stop insisting he learn more about his magic."

What? That was ridiculous. "But why? If he doesn't learn to control it, someone could get hurt. What about what happened to his father? He has to live with that guilt. If he had just known what he was. How to control his power..."

"That wasn't Oliver's real father."

"What? Does Oliver know that?"

Ms. Chase stared at the floor. "No." She looked back at me, pleading in her eyes. "Please. You can't tell him. Oliver's real father is dangerous. That's why I never told Oliver what he really was. About his power. I've tried to keep him hidden from his father." Fear replaced the pleading, and her eyes were wet. "If his father finds out that Oliver is an Elemental..." Her voice trailed off.

"Who is his father? Does he know that Oliver exists? Is he a creature?" The questions came pouring out of me, though I knew I most likely wouldn't get answers to any of them.

"He knows about Oliver, but thinks he has no power. That's why he left. His son is useless to him if he is powerless. I'd like to keep it that way."

"But—"

"Please. Oliver listens to you. I should go. I know you are seeing him soon and I don't want him to know about any of this. It's bad enough that he is questioning if I am an Elemental like he is." Ms. Chase wrapped her arms tightly around herself and went to leave.

"Ms. Chase?"

She stopped in the doorway but didn't turn to face me.

"Oliver means a lot to me. I will do my best to help, but now that he knows what he is..." I shrugged. "Maybe send him to school here? We could keep him hidden. No one would suspect him to be here if they don't know about his magic."

She stood there for a minute with her back to me, then said over her shoulder, "Please don't say anything to Oliver." With that, she slid out the door.

Chapter 17

A dark cloud forced its way into my mind. How was I supposed to keep a secret this big from Oliver? How could his own mother keep it from him? Part of me wanted to tell him everything as soon as I picked him up on the old bridge half an hour later.

But the rational part of me understood the need to keep the secret. I didn't want to put him in any danger. I would have to hold my tongue. For now, at least. Oliver was supposed to have another session with Dr. Winter, but now that his mother was intent on him not learning more about wielding the elements, I suddenly felt like I should have canceled the lesson.

But as soon as I laid eyes on Oliver standing in our meeting spot on the bridge, I knew that he needed this. His eyes were distant and pensive as he watched the smooth current of the river below, and I could tell he was still processing all of the changes to his world since he met me.

Even if his mother didn't want him to learn more, he needed to understand what he was. And I was going to help him through it. No matter what we might have to face when the truth finally came out.

▲ ▲ ▲ ▲

So, there we were. Back in the greenhouse with Dr. Winter, but this time there was no pot of water or plant on the professor's table in the back of the building. Instead, he walked us to the other end and stopped in front of a Strangler Fig tree. The tree was monstrous and loomed angrily about 20 feet above our heads.

Both Oliver and I strained our necks to see to the top of the plant and, just like the first time, I heard his pulse flowing rapidly through his veins as Oliver's anxiety increased.

"I've given your case a lot of thought since the last time we met, Mr. Chase." Dr Winter stared up at the Strangler Fig next to us and placed a hand on Oliver's shoulder. "Control is what you lack. And as anger and stress seem to cause you to react quickly, and powerfully, I thought it would be a good idea to teach you how to stop the elements after calling upon them."

The professor moved to the far side of the tree and patted its enormous trunk. "This is a Strangler Fig. It preys on other trees by growing around them and 'strangling' them, cutting off their sunlight and invading their root systems. What you are looking at was once a large palm. It has now become a host to the Fig."

Oliver reached for my hand, maybe for support. "So, what am I supposed to do with it? Stop it from growing over the palm?"

"No, I'm afraid it's too late for the host plant. I want to see if you can stop the Fig's trunk from growing."

"I don't understand. If it has already killed the palm, why is it still growing?" I could feel Oliver's palm grow slick in my grip and I gave him a little squeeze of encouragement.

"Just focus on your stress. I want you to think of the same image you thought of the other day. But channel it to the trunk of this Fig." Dr. Winter glanced at me briefly. "You will see where you need to focus your energy to stop it soon enough."

I suddenly got a very bad feeling about this. I tentatively took a step back from the tree and slid into the corner next to Oliver. He looked back at me, a question in his eyes. I simply nodded and he turned back to Dr. Winter.

"Ok, Mr. Chase. Let's begin."

Oliver made a show of stretching his neck and stretched his hands and knuckles in front of himself. "Right. Think of something bad?"

Dr. Winter bobbed his chin in response. "The same thought from our last session."

"Ok, but it would be a shame to break all of the windows again." Oliver closed his eyes and winced slightly. A low groaning sound filled the greenhouse, and I watched in stunned amazement as the tree's trunk split into multiple branches, slowly spreading, and reaching across the floor. Oliver's eyes were still shut, and his chest heaved as whatever he was thinking was upsetting him more and more by the second.

The Fig grew faster, its root-like trunk crawling and stretching out, grabbing at, and curling itself around anything in its path. I backed further into the corner as it began to branch out in my direction.

"Oliver." I panicked, backing up into the corner as much as I could before hitting the glass wall of the greenhouse. "Oliver!"

Oliver opened his eyes and immediately went into panic mode. "Cali!" He tried fighting the growing roots, pulling back on them, stomping on them. He spun to see Dr. Winter mid-air, tangled in one of the Fig's giant trunks. "Dr. Winter! I don't know what to do!" yelled Oliver.

Dr. Winter wriggled in the tree's tight grip. "Focus on telling the plant to stop growing." His voice was strained with the ever-tightening roots. "Think. About what. Gets you...upset...or. Nervous." Dr. Winter's face began turning an ugly shade of purple.

"Oliver!" I screamed again, the roots winding around my legs and torso. "Help!"

Oliver's heart was racing so hard and loudly I thought he might have a heart attack and we would all die there in the greenhouse. He climbed over the tree's trunk that covered the floor and tried to pry it off from around my arms. "I'll get you out. Just. I'm going to get this off..."

The roots were squeezing me so tightly, I could barely breathe anymore. I really didn't want to die like this. I was only nineteen. And I just started this thing with Oliver. I had to help him use his power.

"Oliver. You have to tell the tree to. Stop." Talking was getting more and more difficult, the vines tightening around me with every breath I drew.

Tears streamed down his perfect face. "I can't. I don't know how."

"Yes. You do. Focus...on what...makes you. Happ—" My voice trailed off and the periphery of my vision got all fuzzy. This was it. I was going to die. I fought against the ensuing doom, trying to keep conscious. Oliver held my face in his hands, his eyes closed. He whispered something and kissed my lips just before my world turned black.

***

My head was pounding, and it felt like I had been run over by a dozen trucks. Twice. My eyelids fluttered open, and I was staring up at the glass ceiling of the greenhouse. Everything was cloudy and started to spin, forcing me to shut my eyes tight for a few seconds.

"Calina?" Oliver's voice floated over me, and I felt a warm hand on my cheek.

I blinked my eyes again and tried to focus on his face to keep the rest of the world from spiraling around me. Oliver let out an exhale and his breaths came hard and fast as he stared down at me.

"Calina! Thank goodness. I...I don't know what happened. I'm so sorry. I could have..." He trailed off and his eyes glistened with moisture.

"Where's Dr. Winter?" My voice didn't sound like my own and I groaned against the nausea and dizziness plaguing me. I slowly made the transition from the floor to my forearms, pausing to allow the tiny stars to fade from my vision.

"He's fine. He went to get help. Here, let me." He helped me to sit up, clutching my hand in his with an almost painful squeeze.

I squeezed his hand back and reached out, only for Oliver to back away from my touch. He held his head in his hands and rested his elbows on his knees.

"Oliver—" I reached for him again.

"You could have died."

"It wasn't your fault."

His head jerked up and he stared at me with such intensity that I inched away from him instinctively. "It's not my fault? How can you say that? Look around, you!" Anger burned in his beautiful brown eyes as he swept an arm out to his side like a model on a gameshow revealing the grand prize. But in this case, the prize was shorn tree trunks and scuffed tile.

His expression terrified me, and I lowered my voice in hopes of calming his bubbling rage. We certainly didn't need another "incident" from his growing emotions. Plus, if any blame needed to be placed, then it should have all been directed at me.

"Oliver, it was an accident. You'll learn to control it. We just need—"

He stood abruptly. "We need to stop this."

"Wha--? What are you saying? It just takes time to learn..." I slowly pushed myself up from the tile floor, staggering slightly as a wave of dizziness washed over me. Oliver took ahold of my elbow to steady me, then quickly released me the moment I stopped swaying.

He backed away from me, his hands in his pockets. "This is too much. I don't want to hurt anybody...you almost...we can't do this anymore. I can't do this anymore."

"Listen, I know things got a little out of control today, but you did stop it. Eventually." Given, me and Dr. Winter *had* almost died. Semantics.

Oliver shook his head. "I didn't stop the tree. I couldn't."

"I did."

We both jumped at the deep voice that came from behind us. Headmaster Simon strolled through the fallen Fig vines that were still scattered all over the floor of the greenhouse, gingerly stepping over large pieces of root before coming to a halt in front of us. "To be more accurate, I tore through the Fig's vines to free Dr. Winter. And *he* stopped the weed from growing."

Shit. I inched closer to Oliver and tried to take his hand, but he was hell bent on keeping them stuffed in his pockets. I could hear his heartbeat quicken as Headmaster Simon towered over us in his massive werewolf form. Oliver must have been terrified.

I know I was.

Headmaster Simon didn't look pleased. Or fazed. He adjusted his shirt cuffs under his expensive suit jacket as he assessed the destruction of the greenhouse. Finally, after what seemed like an eternity of the Headmaster staring us both down, he spoke again.

"I usually do not question the lectures or teaching styles of my Professors, but I think in this case, I need to inquire about it." His dark emerald eyes looked Oliver up and down. "Especially when we have visitors that I was unaware were invited."

"Headmaster, I—" I tried to explain myself. The situation. But he cut me off before I got the chance.

"Miss Strovsky, correct?"

I nodded.

"You do understand the rules of this Academy, do you not?"

"Yes sir, but—"

"Then you already know that inviting those who are not..." he paused, considering his next choice of words, "students...is forbidden. That is without my approval, of course."

"Yes, but—" Dammit. I couldn't get in a word with this guy.

"Then you also already know that bringing in a new student who has considerable potential and trying to hide that someone from me is frowned upon." The large wolf let a toothy grin spread on his snout and he held out an impossibly large paw toward Oliver. "I'm Headmaster Simon. I am pleased to meet you. And intrigued."

What? I turned to Oliver who appeared to be just as shocked as I was. Maybe it wasn't shock but complete fear of the beast donning an overpriced Prada suit who addressed him.

Oliver didn't reach out to shake the Headmaster's paw and swallowed hard as he stared at the creature, completely frozen.

The Headmaster lowered his paw. "I'm terribly sorry. Where are my manners? I imagine that seeing me in this state must be horrifying to, well, someone who's new here."

Headmaster Simon stood perfectly straight, closing his eyes in concentration. Oliver and I were motionless as we witnessed him transform into his human form. His stature shortened and his thick black hair remained on his head but thinned and disappeared over his smooth, rich brown skin of his arms and face. His snout reshaped into a slightly pointed nose and a chiseled jawline. His eyes were the same intense green as they had been in his werewolf form, and he smiled when his transition was complete.

I stared with my mouth slightly open as I witnessed his transformation. Headmaster Simon was kind of hot.

"There now. Let's try this again." He stuck out his hand to Oliver once more. "Pleasure."

Oliver arched an eyebrow and I really wished that I had the same mind reading power as Shani. He cautiously extended his hand, shaking the Headmaster's. "I'm Oliver. It's nice to meet you, Sir."

I attempted to intercept the conversation once more. "Headmaster, I'm so sorry about this. We were working with Dr. Winter on Oliver's abilities. It got out of hand, and—"

"Yes, Miss Strovsky, you were both very fortunate that I made my rounds when I did." The Headmaster looked around the wrecked greenhouse again. "Young man, this was a dangerous experiment. What if I hadn't walked by? Would you have been able to control this?" He gestured to the overgrown vines that nearly killed me earlier.

Oliver winced and he stared at the floor. "I don't know. I literally just found out that I have these abilities, or whatever, a few weeks ago." I went to reach for his hand again and he stepped away, putting his hands in his pockets.

"I see." Headmaster Simon tilted his head to the side. "I have seen powers like this before, but I'm afraid it's been too long. I would love for you to stay at the Academy. Let me help you figure out how to utilize these...abilities."

Oliver looked back up to Headmaster Simon. "I'm not sure I want to figure out how to use them. How am I supposed to learn how to control myself without putting everyone in danger? Someone's going to get hurt because of me."

"Possibly. But someone will definitely get hurt if you refuse to try. You may have just realized that you have this power but ignoring it will not make it go away." Headmaster Simon searched Oliver's face as if remembering or recognizing something in him. "It's uncanny..." His voice trailed off and he refocused on Oliver. "Think about it. In the meantime, I suggest that you and Miss Strovsky exit the greenhouse so Dr. Winter and I can get things back in order."

I didn't wait for Oliver to respond and looped my arm through his, leading him to the door. "Thank you, Headmaster."

"Oh, and Miss Strovsky?"

Great. I swung around, Oliver still in tow. "Yes, Sir?"

"I trust that another incident like this one will never happen again." Headmaster Simon gave me a tight-lipped smile that didn't reach his eyes. Even though the man was incredibly handsome, his expression in that particular moment was chilling.

I swallowed hard and nodded before leading Oliver out the door at a quicker pace than before. My grip tightened around his arm, and we raced away from the greenhouse in silence.

In fact, the entire car ride was silent as Oliver simply stared out of the passenger seat window while I drove him back into town. I tried to hold his hand to thwart any negative thoughts that might still be lingering about what had happened tonight. But he just subtly pulled his arms to his chest, crossing them in front of him, completely shutting me out.

I didn't press him and kept on driving toward the old bridge. When we arrived, he got out of the car so quickly that I practically fell out of the driver's side and had to jog after him down the cobblestone street.

"Oliver, wait!" I grabbed his hand to slow his exit. He turned around but refused to look me in the eye. I took both of his hands in mine. "Oliver, please, things will get better. You heard Headmaster Simon. You can come to the Academy. Learn how to use your magic."

He still didn't look at me and his face was hard as stone. I stood on my tiptoes, placing my hands on his cheeks, and forcing him to meet my eye. "I'm ok. No one was hurt. I know you're scared, but I'll be here to help. Oliver, please look at me."

His brown eyes darkened but he finally looked at me. I smiled slightly. "We can do this together." I waited for him to respond and grew hopeful when he leaned in and rested his forehead to mine. "Besides, now we're even, right?" His eyes flashed and I immediately regretted my poor attempt at lightening the mood.

"I can't." His hands cupped my face and his lips brushed against mine so quickly that I might have imagined it. Then he turned and started back down the street.

"What happened to 'dangerous or not, you're not going anywhere'?" I yelled to his back, against the growing lump in my throat.

He paused for a moment, shoulders slumping, then continued along the dark alley toward his home.

Chapter 18

Oliver hadn't returned my calls or texts for over a week, and I didn't see him on his porch reading while I spent the weekend at dad's.

He was actively avoiding me.

And I was actively acting like a typical college student, listening to emo rock bands and feeling sorry for myself. Even "creature watching" on my bench in the middle of campus had lost its luster. Not to mention, I was now teetering on failing my Vampire Arts class. I wondered if I could use compulsion on Ms. Dunning to make her change my grade to an A.

Of course, if I was able to use compulsion on another vampire, I would have probably been making an A already.

I exhaled dramatically and rested my head against the hard stone of the bench. A group of tiny pixies fluttered around my head, chattering obnoxiously. I swatted at them with my hand as if they were a hoard of insects and one stuck her tongue out at me before their group flew away.

"Wow, swatting at a group of pixies? Bold move. Also, kind of mean." Shani didn't look up from her textbook that was sprawled over her lap. "Look, I know you miss Oliver, but geez. That is not an excuse to pick on tiny creatures. Even if they are incredibly annoying." She sighed. "Just call him already."

"I've tried. He won't respond to any of my calls." I folded my arms over my chest like a pouting child. I did feel kind of bad about the pixies.

"The pixies will get over it. And so will Oliver. Give him time. It had to be horrifying to almost kill the person you're in love with."

What?

She still didn't look up at me. "You heard me."

"Stop with the mind reading. And he isn't in love with me. I mean, I'm sure he cares about me but—"

"The boy is head over heels. And so are you. So just go find him and be done with this drama already." Shani rolled her eyes to the pages in her textbook. "It's such a buzz kill."

I laughed and nudged her shoulder. "Ok. I'll stop being 'such a buzz kill'." Suddenly, doubt infiltrated and crushed my vision of a happy reunion with Oliver. "What if he doesn't want to see me ever again?" I almost whispered.

"Impossible. You're amazing. Besides, you almost killed him too so it's not like it's a one-sided thing. You are both equally dangerous to the other. And equally perfect together." She shrugged. "Just my opinion."

I smiled and pulled her in for a one-armed side hug. "Thanks. You're pretty amazing too."

Shani leaned into my hug. "I know. Now go to class before you get kicked out for being tardy."

Shani was right. I was almost ten minutes late for Vampire Arts. Between hovering at a D+ and not listening to her dangerous Elemental warning, I was batting a thousand with Ms. Dunning. I rushed from the bench and bolted straight to the Magical Arts building and into class.

Ms. Dunning was in the middle of lecture and scowled at me as I sneaked in the door and to the back of the classroom. She continued her presentation on balance and bloodlust, and I sighed in relief that she wasn't going to point out my rudeness in front of the class.

When the lecture was over, Ms. Dunning motioned for me to approach her desk as the other students filed out of the room. I waited for everyone else to exit then waited for her to tell me how annoyed she was at my tardiness. But she didn't mention it.

"I heard about what happened the other night in the greenhouse. I thought I advised you to stop this mission of helping your friend with his power."

That was unexpected. "You did. But I can't. I have to help him. It is who he is, and he needs to learn how to control himself." Oliver *did* need to accept his magic. Even if he didn't want my help in doing so, I was still going to be there for him. This was the third time I was cautioned to watch my back from some random Elemental. Once from my mother, and now twice from my professor. What were they so afraid of?

"Calina, please, you don't understand who you're—" Ms. Dunning abruptly cut herself off and smiled sweetly toward the door behind me.

Headmaster Simon knocked as he entered the classroom. "Ms. Dunning, a word?" He was in his werewolf form, and he flashed a toothy grin at me when he noticed that I was standing there. "Ah, Miss Strovsky. Nice to see you. Again."

Ms. Dunning nodded then cleared her throat. "I will see you for your tutoring session next week, Miss Strovsky."

She dismissed me. "Yes, ma'am, but—"

Her eyes widened and she gave a subtle shake of her head alerting me to stop talking. I obeyed. "See you next week." I nodded to Dr. Simon, "Nice to see you, Headmaster," then I quickly slipped out of the classroom, feeling both of their stares on me until I was well down the hallway.

△ △ △ △

I waited in front of Oliver's house for almost two hours. Well, I watched his house from a couple houses down the block. His mom was pretty intimidating, and I didn't want to chance another run in with her. He had to come home eventually.

I paced back and forth along the uneven cobblestone path, my hands wringing together so tightly that my knuckles were white, and my palms were damp. If I wasn't overly anxious before, I certainly was now that I was confronted about getting too involved in the Elemental arena. Again.

After another thirty minutes, I decided that it might be a lost cause and headed back toward the center of town. It was probably safer for us to stay apart. That was what I told myself anyway, but as I approached the old bridge, I was flooded with images of my first date with Oliver. His perfect smile. Our "almost" kiss. I wandered to the stone railing and watched the river peacefully flow beneath me.

Who was I kidding? I would have chanced fighting a thousand fig trees and all-powerful bad guys if it meant I could be with Oliver. Too bad he didn't feel the same.

"Calina?"

I spun on my heel to see Oliver waving to me from the opposite end of the bridge. I let my now sweaty palms fall to my side and attempted a smile.

He all but ran toward me and immediately wrapped his arms around my waist, lifting me off the ground in, an almost too tight, embrace. When he lowered me back down, he buried his face into my neck. "I'm so sorry," he mumbled.

I pulled away from him so I could see his face. "You've been avoiding me. I went to your house to talk...I waited..." I looked at my feet. Half of me wanted to stay wrapped up in his arms, but the more logical half was still hurt at how he had left things the other night.

"I know, and I'm sorry. For everything. This is just new for me. And, if I'm being honest, I'm scared to death. Not just about how I could hurt you, but that I care so much. About you." His eyes were amber under the afternoon sun as he searched mine. "You mean the world to me, Cali. And it scares the hell out of me."

I forced my face to stay neutral, fighting against the warmth that was flooding my cheeks. I wasn't going to give in that easily. "You really hurt me that night. I only wanted to help you." I bit my lip to keep from pulling him in for a kiss. Damn, he made it near impossible to stand my ground.

His hands settled on my hips, and he drew me into him, so our faces were nearly touching. "You did help. You are. Let me make it up to you, and I promise I won't be so stupid again." He didn't wait for me to accept his apology or question his promise and his lips met mine with a fever.

Screw it.

I relished the feeling of his mouth against mine and wanted to remain frozen in that moment forever. I only broke away from his hold when heavy raindrops fell on our heads from a clear blue sky.

We both lifted our heads to scan the cloudless sky while getting soaked from the rain that Oliver had unintentionally created. I thought he might get nervous, but he surprised me when that beautiful grin lit up his face just before pressing his lips to mine again.

I let him lead me back down the cobblestone path to his little cottage, and I paused briefly considering if I wanted to see his mother again. I didn't have to wonder long, however, because Oliver tucked me under his arm and whispered, "no one is home." I could practically hear the sly smile in his voice as his lips brushed lightly against my ear. My breath hitched and a rush of excitement flowed through me.

Before I knew it, I was following Oliver over the threshold of his front door, our fingers laced tightly together. A heartbeat later, he pushed me up against the wall of the foyer, his hands gripping my waist and his body pressed into me. I wrapped my arms around his neck and found his lips with mine, playfully nibbling his bottom lip as I fell into his kiss. Our clothes were still soaked from Oliver's rainstorm, and I let him peel off my shirt and toss it to the floor with a satisfying plunk. He then reached down and pulled off his wet polo shirt, his muscular abdomen tensing with the movement.

I stared at his taught chest, suddenly needing to explore every inch of it. I ran my fingernails down his chest, and he emitted a low growl, lifting me off of the ground. I wrapped my thighs around his waist and let my hands run through his thick brown hair. He grasped onto my thighs and carried me across the living room and into his bedroom.

Oliver carefully lowered me onto his bed, my legs still wound around him. He kissed my lips so gingerly then stared into my eyes, his hands resting on the bed on either side of my shoulders. "You're perfect."

My cheeks burned and his gaze was so intense yet vulnerable, that I pulled his face down to mine, meeting his lips with a passion I had never experienced before. Being with him. Kissing him in that moment was even more euphoric than the taste of his blood during our last tryst.

His hands roved softly along my stomach and down to my hips. His fingers trailed over the hem of my skirt and his eyes met mine in question. I gave him a slight nod and he leaned down to kiss me again while his hands easily pulled my skirt down before unbuttoning his own pants. His talented fingers then teased my center, circling over and inside of me and I moaned in anticipation. I nearly screamed out, but my cry was smothered when Oliver's mouth pressed hard to mine again. His lips roamed lower along my throat, and he kissed his way down to my chest, making a detour to taste my nipples before traveling to my navel, then, finally between my legs.

My back arched off of the bed at the feeling of his mouth, his tongue flitting and twirling against me. I clutched at the pillows and cried out before reaching for his shoulders to pull him back to me. I couldn't take the torture of his teasing for one more second and was about to explode from the heat and pleasure building inside of my body. I needed to feel all of him.

He sensed my need and teased me longer, his tongue moving in unison and just above his fingers. I gasped and my ragged breaths hitched around another cry of ecstasy. This time, I sat up and pulled his face back up to mine and he bit my bottom lip as he slid into me. It was all I could do to not burst into flames at the amazing feeling of his length pulsing within me.

Our bodies were a perfect fit with one another, and we moved in a harmonious rhythm that grew in intensity and passion. My nails gripped into Oliver's lower back, and I tightened around his length as I peaked. He moaned at the feeling of my climax and his movement slowed and deepened as he reached his own end.

We lie there for several minutes, skin to skin, panting lightly in the afterglow of the paradise we had created together. Oliver rolled to his side and wrapped his arm around my bare waist, pulling me as close to him as possible. He held me there for a moment, his face buried in my neck before rotating onto his back. I turned to my side resting my head on my hand watching him as he rested next to me with his eyes closed peacefully.

Oliver wasn't the first guy I had been that intimate with, but he was certainly in the lead for being the best. As if he had heard my thoughts, a lazy smile spread on his lips and I rested my head back down on his chest, feeling the slight rise and fall of his relaxed breathing.

He laid his arm over mine, absently stroking my shoulder with his fingers, and planting a light kiss on the top of my head. "You didn't bite me."

I smiled and wrapped my leg around his. "You didn't cause a fire. Or tornado. Or—"

"Ha. Okay, I get it." He took my chin and tilted my head to look at him. "I think I was too focused on you. I wasn't nervous. Or scared. And it was like just being with you...distracted me somehow." He leaned down to kiss the top of my nose and I nuzzled my face comfortably into his chest again.

"You can put all of that focus on me anytime." I smiled against his beating heart, recalling the immense pleasure that he had wrought from me only moments earlier.

"I will definitely take you up on that." He returned to idly stroking his fingers along my shoulder. As we lie there in silence, the world melted away, and just for the night, I allowed myself to not think about magic or schools or bad guys, only the perfection of being in Oliver's arms.

Chapter 19

I had never been more excited about a school sporting event than I was that afternoon while getting ready for the lacrosse game against Freyshire. As we applied our makeup, Shani was talking a mile a minute about her date from the bar, Sarah. Apparently, she wasn't only a server who was the one who invented Blood Orange Martinis but was also the starting Attacker on St. Anne's lacrosse team. St. Anne's was more than progressive when it came to coed college level sports. Maybe that was partly due to the fact that *all* students had special abilities, so there was no need to segregate genders.

Not that they were allowed to use said abilities in games. I didn't think they did, anyway.

Shani was bummed about not having someone to sit with in the stands, but I knew she was secretly excited to be the girl who ran on the field and ran into a sweaty embrace with her star player.

"Are you even listening to me?" Shani paused mid lipstick application and stared at me in the mirror. "And I will *not* be giving Sarah a sweaty hug." She shuddered at the thought and rolled her eyes before returning to her lipstick.

"I'm sorry. I'm just a little preoccupied. You should have seen us, Shani. It was like something out of a romance novel." I swooned, recalling my kiss in the rain with Oliver.

"Trust me, it's like I was there. That's all you've been thinking about the last couple of days." She made a disgusted face at herself in the mirror.

I wondered how much of my night she "saw", and I should have scolded her for intruding on my personal thoughts again, but, honestly, I didn't care.

Everything was too perfect. Oliver was amazing and cheering for him at the game was going to be a blast.

▲▲▲▲

The only stadium in Freyshire was a multi-purpose field. It was what the few colleges in the area used for their home sporting events of lacrosse, soccer, and the occasional rugby game. It was probably the most modern looking building in the entire town with gray cement block and stucco surrounding the all-turf field. The biggest contrast was the paved road and surrounding parking lots that made it stick out like a sore thumb in a village of cobblestone and brown brick.

The entrance gates were black iron and towered a good twenty feet above the cement walkway. They seemed a bit out of place, but I supposed taller gates were useful when metal detectors had to be fit in the entryway somehow.

"Look! There's Sarah!" Shani pointed to a tall player practicing tosses with another player on the sidelines. Sarah stopped for a moment and glanced in our direction, grinning wide and waving to Shani, her large fangs extended for all to see. "I'm going to go say hi before the game." Shani glanced at me, "Reema and I will meet you at our seats." She motioned for Reema to follow her and Reema begrudgingly left me alone to find Oliver.

He and the Freyshire team were tossing balls back and forth and doing running drills on the opposite side of the stadium. I spotted him on the bench, tightening his shoelaces and he glanced in my direction, a huge smile forming on his lips when he saw me. He looked incredibly adorable in his white uniform and elbow pads, and he stuck his helmet under his arm as he jogged over to me.

His arms immediately curled around my waist, and he planted a kiss on my forehead. "Hi." I returned the embrace, taking in his Christmassy scent.

Oliver nodded toward Shani talking to Sarah across the field, and whispered, "Is she a vampire like you?" He narrowed his eyes and briefly glanced at my mouth as if expecting to see my own fangs.

"Why? Scared?" I giggled and shook my head. "No. She's most likely a werewolf. They aren't able to hide their fangs like us. Vampires, I mean."

"Right." His brow furrowed, lost in thought.

"What is it?"

"Nothing. It's just. Didn't your Headmaster pull his fangs in? And he's a werewolf, right?" Oliver shrugged and shook his head, pulling me in tighter to his chest. "What do I know? I was just a normal human a couple months ago."

I buried my face into his chest. Headmaster Simon *was* a werewolf. But he also was able to retract his fangs...something only vampires could do. I vaguely remembered him pulling in his sharp canines at the St. Anne's orientation, but I must have been too nervous to give it another thought. It made absolutely no sense. I wondered...

I was pulled out of my head and back onto the field when Oliver stepped out of our embrace, eyes roving around the stadium. His eyes lit up beneath the bright lights as if he were seeing the world for the very first time. He kind of was. "This is insane. I mean, the fact that your school's student body is comprised of creatures is, well, unbelievable. But this." He gestured his arms wide in front of him and looked like he might implode from excitement at any minute. "Is that an ogre? It's like my eyes are finally open. Why couldn't I see this before?"

I shrugged. "Yep. But no one in the stands can see his true form but creatures. St. Anne's is pretty good at keeping the backgrounds of its students a secret from the general public."

"Magic?" He raised an eyebrow suspiciously.

I winked in response, then surveyed the lacrosse field and stands that surrounded it. And I had to admit, it was pretty cool. The students from St. Anne's had taken over the left half of the bleachers, all sporting their red and black and waving foam fingers and "Go Bulls" flags while screaming at the top of their lungs. Then, of course, the Freyshire College students were cheering on the opposite side, with a little less flair and noise, but still waving flags adorned in their school's colors of blue and gray.

I placed a hand on Oliver's shoulder and tilted my chin back to the sidelines where the team from Freyshire College was warming up. "You better go get ready for your game."

He nodded and wrapped his arm around my shoulders, pulling me into him. He kissed my temple. "Wish me luck."

I blushed. "Good luck."

He smirked. "I mean, knowing what I do now about the opposing team, this game feels a bit unfair."

"You'll be fine." I gave him a customary pat on the behind as he jogged off to rejoin his team. He looked back at me over his shoulder, a sly smile on his lips.

I watched Oliver run to the opposite side of the field then decided I should find my seat before the stadium got too packed. I strode up the endless concrete steps to our seats directly in line with the field goal post. Shani waved frantically to me and Reema patted an open spot between them. We watched the game excitedly, all three of us cheering for both sides whenever our star players made a good play.

Shani smiled and dreamily stared at the field, leaning her head on my shoulder. "Look at our adorable lacrosse players."

I laughed at her and rested my head on hers. "They are pretty cute."

"Bleh. You both are disgusting." Reema stuck her tongue out and shivered dramatically. "I'm going to go grab a drink." Shani and I giggled to each other as Reema carefully stepped down the steep concrete steps in her three-inch heels.

We returned to watching the game, and when the clock chimed that it was halftime, the score was tied 5-5. The two teams went to their respective sidelines and were drinking Gatorade and resting on the benches. Oliver took off his helmet and looked up to where I was sitting. He grinned and waved at me before grabbing his water bottle. His cheeks were pink, and his hair was a sweaty mess and all I could think about was how much I wanted to have a repeat of the other night in my car.

Without the almost killing him part.

My face flushed hot at the thought of the two of us tangled up in each other and I couldn't stop smiling.

Until I saw Reema walking over to where he and the other players were sitting. She waved to Oliver and beckoned him over to the fence. She settled her arms on the metal railing, her breasts practically falling out over it as she leaned in towards the field.

I tried not to vomit in the stands as I watched Oliver walk toward Reema, her sparkling smile spreading seductively on her full lips.

"What is Reema doing?" Shani stared at her sister.

"Reema said something about some chemistry question she just *had* to ask Oliver. I didn't think she meant right now, at this very minute." I rolled my eyes and crossed my arms tightly over my chest.

"I wouldn't worry. Oliver is completely nuts about you," Shani assured me while keeping her eyes on Reema.

"I know," I said, still sick to my stomach while watching Reema toss her hair and laugh like Oliver had just said the most hilarious thing.

Shani nudged me. "You should go talk to him for a minute before halftime ends."

Sounded like a great excuse for a quick kiss. "Come with me?"

"Can we buy a soda on the way?"

I nodded and we made our way down the treacherous bleachers to the concession stand. Shani suddenly walked as close as she could to me, and lowered her voice to ask, "I meant to ask you...what did Oliver's mother say to you when she came to the dorm?"

I wasn't sure if I should tell her or not. Then again, if I didn't, she would have just pried it from my thoughts later.

"Exactly. So just tell me."

I scowled at her. "You swear you won't say anything? To anyone?" I waited for her to nod in affirmation then relayed my conversation with Oliver's mom. "I really want to tell Oliver. But. What if something happened to him? Because of me? I mean, obviously his mom would know just how dangerous his father is."

"Who *is* his real father? Did she tell you?"

"No. She didn't say a name, and she looked terrified to be seen at the school. It was like she was nervous someone might recognize her?" I shook my head to myself. "I don't know. The whole thing is just weird."

"Well, you can't tell Oliver the truth about the guy he thought was his dad." Shani chewed on her bottom lip. "But I think we are a little late on the whole 'not telling him about his magic' thing. He already knows. And he's been exposed to the creature side of Freyshire."

"I know." I sighed and wrapped my arms around myself. The air was getting cooler by the minute and a steady breeze lifted the hair from my shoulders.

"We need to figure out who this scary mystery man is."

I glanced at her and opened my mouth to respond but was interrupted by a strong gust of wind that hit me in the face. I searched the parking lot near the concession stand and watched as soda bottles and trash were blown around the patrons. The crowd didn't seem to notice the miniature hurricane brewing inside the stadium and just cheered that much louder when a bolt of lightning flashed through the sky above the field. The marching band was in the middle of their routine and their drumming grew in intensity to compete with the ensuing storm.

Shani's eyes widened and she seemed to be thinking the same thing that I was, and I made a beeline for the field. "Something's wrong. I need to find Oliver."

I raced back toward the sidelines where Oliver and his team were resting up for the second half of the game. Shani was yelling something from behind me, but I knew she was following me, so I didn't turn back. The wind was whipping against my face, stinging my cheeks and eyes but no amount of wind could've blocked me from the sight in front of me.

I stopped short, hot tears stinging the sides of my eyes. There, standing at the edge of the sideline fence, were Oliver and Reema. But I could only see their profiles since they were tangled up in what appeared to be a passionate kiss.

I rubbed my eyes. Closed them tight and reopened them, hoping that I was somehow imagining the whole thing. My throat burned and I choked back the tears as I watched her hands claim him like he belonged to her. His hand rested gently on her cheek and brushed a piece of hair behind her ear. Like he always did with me. Their shared embrace was a moment so intimate that I almost felt like I shouldn't be staring.

Except for the fact that Oliver was *my* boyfriend.

How could he? With Reema?

Shani stopped right next to me. "Reema!" The anger in her voice sounded off of the metal bleachers behind us and I wouldn't have wanted to be on the receiving end of it.

Reema and Oliver pulled away from each other, and Reema gazed at me with a smirk on her lips. Oliver's eyes narrowed slightly at Reema then turned into a look of terror when he saw me. He glanced between me and Reema, then raced toward me.

"Cali? I...what?" His hands shot up to the sides of his head as if severely confused.

I backed away, shaking my head and trying to hold back the tears. He didn't deserve to see me upset. And I didn't want to hear any of his would-be excuses. Or apologies. None of it would change what I had just witnessed.

Even if his expression was laced with anguish.

I didn't care. I turned around and walked away from him. From all of them. I kept walking, ignoring the shouts from Oliver for me to come back.

I started running and kept going until I was safely a block away from the stadium. When I was sure that no one had followed me, I slowed my pace and dropped onto the curb. I buried my head into my lap, allowing the ugly tears to flow.

What the hell happened? How could we go from the most perfect kiss to him making out with my archenemy? Ok, arch-enemy was a bit of an exaggeration, but seriously, Reema? I wiped the flood waters pouring from my eyes and peered up at the full moon shining down.

I decided it was a good time to see dad. Usually, a break-up situation was more my mom's territory, but, honestly, I didn't feel like going into detail or hearing the old "I told you so". Plus, it was the night of the Wild Hunt, so I knew dad would be busy partying and eating souls, or whatever him and his friends did during the hunt. But it seemed like a good place to hide out for the weekend.

Chapter 20

I no sooner arrived at my dad's when my phone started blowing up. First it was Oliver. Then Shani. I thought about answering Shani's call but turned my phone on silent instead. I stuffed it in my pocket and stared out of my bedroom window toward the house that I had basically stalked for months.

But Oliver wasn't there. I didn't want him to be.

I closed my eyes, leaning against the glass and when I opened them again, Oliver was standing on his porch. His beautiful brown eyes dark and sad. He waved and held up his phone and signaled for me to do the same. I knew I shouldn't. But I pulled my phone from my pocket and answered his call when it came through.

"Cali, please hear me out. I had no idea—"

Nope. I changed my mind. I couldn't listen to this. "You had no idea that I would see you?" My voice was shaky, and anger surged through me. I hoped he could feel the daggers darting from my eyes that I mentally threw in his direction.

His expression was pained, and I could almost feel the agony that radiated from his entire being as he watched me through the window. "No. That's not what I was going to say. Cali, I'm sorry. It was an accident!"

"You just accidentally made out with my roommate?" I sarcastically threw my free hand in the air. "Yeah, ok. Sure." I hardened my expression. He looked miserable. Wasn't my problem.

"Calina—" He practically begged.

"No. This is insane. I should have known that this was going to happen. I just thought you were different. I thought...you know what? It doesn't matter. Don't call me again." I hung up the phone and turned away from the window. I ran from the room, hot tears streaming down my cheeks, and raced through the long dark hallway toward to the courtyard.

I needed some air. And a drink.

But what had I expected? I shouldn't have even answered the phone in the first place.

▲▲▲▲

The entire weekend flew by in an instant. I had hoped for some time to think. About what had happened between Oliver and

Reema. About the whole "mystery father who might be evil" thing. But it felt like as soon as I had arrived at my dad's place after the game on Friday, it was Sunday evening a minute later.

I also thought that the Wild Hunt would allow me some alone time in the castle, but it was quite the opposite. There were nonstop feasts and celebrations, and my dad tried to convince me to come on the ride with everyone to help distract me. And how could I say no to that? I was never allowed to go before.

Needless to say, I didn't get much time to myself to do the necessary soul searching I had been looking forward to. Shani must have texted me a dozen times, and, though I told him not to, Oliver left me multiple voicemails. All of which I immediately deleted without listening to or reading. I wasn't trying to ignore Shani. But I wasn't ready to talk about the incident yet.

I mean, Oliver made out with Reema. *Reema.*

And it wasn't just him kissing her that bothered me. It was the idea that he was mine. That we were somehow perfect together. And maybe even meant to be together, as much of an idealistic dream that was.

That's what was destroying me.

Tears threatened to ruin my makeup. Ugh. I was so over crying. I swallowed them back and wiped my eyes with the palm of my hands as I packed up my stuff to return to the Academy. I considered staying for the week, but I had a huge exam in Vampire Arts, and I was already doing subpar in that class.

I walked over to my window and stared out to Oliver's house. I think I had hoped to see him there, trying to get my attention. But the porch was empty. Just as it had been since Friday night when he tried to apologize. Again. I rested my forehead against the glass and allowed my pity party to resume.

"Will you be returning to the Academy tomorrow?"

I started at the sound of my father's voice behind me. I turned and gave him a half smile before returning to my packing. "Yeah, I've got an exam this week."

"I see. Good. Remember, straight A's this semester." A tight-lipped smile was on his lips. He had never been that great at the "comforting dad" talks. That was more my mom's thing. But he tried. "You know, it is probably best to not have so many distractions and you'll be able to place all of that energy into your studies. You are better off. In time, you will see." He looked down at his hands that were crossed neatly in front of him.

"You're probably right, dad."

He turned to leave then paused in the doorway, glancing over his shoulder. "You are too good for him anyway."

I melted. I swiped away a tear that had managed to escape and walked over to my dad, wrapping my arms around him. He seemed to freeze a bit but managed to awkwardly pat my arms in a pseudo-hug. "Thanks, dad."

△ △ △ △

Before I knew it, I was standing outside of Reformation Hall staring up at the windows of my dormitory. Eventually, I would have to go up to my room. But not yet. I walked around campus for a while until I ended up at my favorite bench near the fountain. The sirens were out practicing their synchronized swimming and singing, and I allowed myself to get lost in the beautifully haunting song.

I closed my eyes and rested my head on the bench soaking in the crisp mid-November breeze when a soft voice broke my mindfulness exercise.

"Good evening, Calina."

I jolted my head up from the bench, sliding slightly away from Oliver's mother. She was seated on the opposite end of the bench as if she were afraid to get too close to me. Her hands were folded neatly in her lap, and she regarded me with a raised eyebrow. I wondered if the woman ever smiled. Or if she even knew how.

"I'm sure you're wondering why I'm here. I understand you and my son had a disagreement."

"That's one way to put it."

She ignored my sharp tone. "I also understand that he is in love with you."

I opened my mouth to respond, but Ms. Chase held up a hand to stop me.

"Please. This is important." She shifted uncomfortably in her seat. "Because of you, Oliver knows what he is."

"That's—" I started.

"Calina, please let me get this out. He knows what he is now, and that means that others will soon know too. That being said, he needs to be protected. I've thought a lot about what you said about sending him here. To St. Anne's, with you. I think it could work...for a while, anyway. At least until I can be sure that no one is looking for him." She paused and looked at me with a kind of question in her eyes.

"My mom told me about you. That you were schoolmates together here. Would Oliver's father even know to look here for him? If you are an Elemental..." I trailed off, not really knowing what I was even asking. I had no idea who his father was. If he had been a student at St. Anne's too. Or the Professor my mother had warned me to steer clear from.

"Oliver's father believes that his son has no power and has no reason to come looking. Unless someone discovers who Oliver is and alerts his father."

Okay, I had to ask. "Ms. Chase, who is this guy? What does he want that would cause him to harm his own son?" I swallowed nervously but stood my ground and kept eye contact with her.

She wrung her hands together over her lap and stared at the fountain.

"Please. I need to know. Who and what are we dealing with?" I started to reach my hand out to give her a supportive pat on the shoulder, but thought better of it and pulled it back, crossing my arms instead.

Oliver's mom didn't look at me and was quiet for several minutes, and I suddenly felt guilty for asking. Then she turned to me, her brown eyes sharp and glowing amber just like Oliver's.

"His father and I met here at the Academy. He was a professor of Elemental Magic during my last year at St. Anne's. Professor John Rowan." Ms. Chase had a far off look in her eyes. "He was a brilliant man. Handsome. Powerful. I immediately fell head over heels in love with him. It was such a whirlwind romance, looking back at it. We got married soon after I graduated, and everything was perfect...normal.

"Then John changed. Not in the usual sense, where you'd hear of people growing apart or fighting more often. It was a subtle change. He became obsessed with having children. A son, specifically." She laughed to herself, still staring out into the distance. "It sounds like medieval times with royalty, doesn't it?" It was a question that I understood to be rhetorical, and I nodded but stayed silent to hear more.

Ms. Chase continued. "You know that Oliver has three older sisters...and their father was elated at their births, but when Oliver was born. John was over the moon. There wasn't anything about that baby boy that wouldn't have been perfect in his father's eyes."

I was confused. The guy sounded ok so far. Gender obsessed, maybe, but that didn't sound dangerous by any means. "So, what happened?"

"John was overly possessive of Oliver. He took over most of the care for him, outside of feeding...even when I would go to pick up my baby, John would take him from my arms.

Or watch me. I was never alone with Oliver in those first few months. It was as if John were scared that I would take Oliver from him. We argued about it frequently, and I would ask him about his behavior, and he would blow me off, telling me that I was being paranoid.

"But, when Oliver was six months old, John turned forty and his demeanor changed yet again. This time it was drastically different. He grew angry and violent around anyone who would go near Oliver. Including me and my daughters. He didn't practice his magic anymore. He would be on mysterious phone calls in his office until late into the night. I almost thought he was having an affair until I came home from work early to find him meeting with a group of older men. I knew that they were Fae, but I had never seen them before. John was letting them examine Oliver and was thumbing through a small leather-bound book. When I walked in the room, they slammed the book shut and left the house without a word to me.

"I was truly scared. I needed to understand what they wanted with Oliver. So, one night, after John fell asleep, I sneaked into his office and searched around for the book I had seen John share with the Faeries. It was an old book of curses...a detailed journal of sorts." Ms. Chase took a long inhale and looked as if she were contemplating telling me the rest or not.

This time, I did reach over to settle my hand on her forearm. "What kind of curses?"

"The kind that cause creatures to lose their power. Or cause their death."

"But what do those kinds of curses have to do with Oliver?" I swallowed hard knowing the answer to my question as soon as I asked it.

"John was cursed. I'm not sure when or by whom, but according to the journal, his power had been weakening for years and was completely gone by the time he turned forty. The only reversal is to take the power from a child that possessed the same magic. A son." Tears formed in the corners of Ms. Chase's eyes. "Taking back that kind of power would kill Oliver."

Oh no.

I tensed, feeling oddly protective of the guy I was trying to stay mad at. "Did John try and take Oliver's power? How did you get him to believe Oliver didn't have any magical abilities?"

"He did try. That's what he was meeting with the Fae elders about. They were going to read Oliver for elemental magic, and if they sensed any abilities, they would transfer the power from him to John." She shrugged. "So, I intervened. I placed my own kind of curse on my only son. I made it appear as if Oliver had no magic at all, basically burying in deep within him so no one could access his power. Not even Oliver. Clearly, my spell hasn't been strong enough to keep Oliver's magic at bay." Ms. Chase stared off into the distance as if contemplating her choice to cover up her son's magical ability.

"Is that when John left? After Oliver failed the test?"

She nodded. "There was no reason for him to stay once he thought his son couldn't save him. My guess? He went to start a new family in hopes for another son that can break the curse."

"Why are his powers so important to him that he would kill his own child?" I couldn't wrap my head around harming your kid just to keep using magic. It was ridiculous.

"John Rowan was one of the most powerful Elementals that has ever existed. And power like that can make someone do just about anything to keep it." Ms. Chase sighed. "So, now you know." She looked at me, an intensity in her gaze that was unnerving. "Do you now understand why I have kept this from Oliver? I didn't want him to live in fear. Especially from a person that was supposed to love him unconditionally. That's why I remarried as quickly as I could...and Oliver has always known my second husband as his father. Not John."

"I guess, but—"

"And this is why if Oliver were to come here, to St. Anne's, I would need you to help me make sure his magic continues to stay under the radar."

"But Oliver and I. We aren't really..." I stopped myself. We weren't really what? Together? Talking? All of the above? He might have wanted to be with Reema, but did that mean I didn't care about him anymore? Did that mean I wouldn't want him to stay safe?

Ms. Chase seemed to be able to read my thoughts and she reached over and placed a hand on mine. It was the first time she offered any kindness to me at all.

"I know I haven't supported your relationship with Oliver. But I want you to know it was only out of fear for my son's safety. I don't know what happened between the two of you, but I believe you still care deeply about him." The right side of her mouth curved up in a half smile. "I need to know that I have someone here to help keep an eye on him."

I nodded. "I can do that."

"Thank you."

We sat for a moment watching the sirens in the fountain before Ms. Chase broke the silence. "You have no idea the amount of regret and guilt that I have lived with over keeping Oliver's identity from him." She looked me square in the eye. "But I'd do it again. It was the only way to keep him safe."

I was taken aback by her vulnerability and attempted a smile in hopes that it might offer some comfort. "I know."

She squeezed my hand before pulling hers away again, then stood. She started to walk away then turned back to me. "He does love you, you know. You should talk to him." And with that, she was gone.

Chapter 21

I sat there, staring blankly at the fountain again, trying to process everything I had just heard. And the entirety of the last week. As if Oliver making out with my nemesis wasn't bad enough, now I was supposed to just go about my day as if I wasn't suddenly privy to this massive secret?

My head suddenly ached and I leaned forward resting my elbows on my knees. I knew that I eventually had to return to my dorm and face Shani. And Reema. I would have to call Oliver at some point too. I didn't know if I was quite ready for that, but if I was supposed to help keep him safe, I should probably give him a chance to explain without flying off the handle. Maintain some kind of friendship. Or stay acquaintances at the very least.

I heaved a sigh then got to my feet. No time like the present.

I headed over to Reformation Hall and made my way up to my room, a new determination to get this whole mess over with and behind me. I took a deep breath and opened the door, stopping immediately at the sight of hundreds of flowers that were blooming from the crevices in the wood floors and busting through cracks in the walls.

A small gasp escaped my lips, and my eyes followed the trail of gorgeous flowers to the back window where Oliver stood beaming at me.

"Surprise." He gestured to the blooms surrounding him. "Like them? It took me all weekend. There were a couple, um, mishaps." He jerked his chin to a few burnt spots on the floor. "Sorry about your area rug."

"I—How did you even get here?" That was the best response I could muster. Not, holy crap, you made a forest. Or even comment on the blackened spots on the wood floor and holes burned into the rug where small fires had broken out.

"I picked him up and brought him here."

I turned to see Shani coming out of her bedroom.

"I tried to text and call, but you weren't responding." Shani walked over to stand next to Oliver. "You really need to hear his side of things." She peered down at the burn marks on the floor. "Especially since he set my Turkish rug on fire trying to make these flowers for you."

I completely ignored her presence and the rug comment and rounded on Oliver. "What *side*? You were making out with Reema. I'm not sure there is a way to explain that. Where is she anyway?" I crossed my arms over my chest and narrowed my eyes at him. So much for not flying off the handle.

"Reema's at dad's for the week." Shani was rooted in place and nodded to Oliver, maybe encouraging him to continue whatever excuse he had come up with since our phone call on Friday.

He inched toward me, slowly with his hands raised slightly in front of him, as if he might scare me away. As if I was a wounded animal.

I kind of was.

"Cali, I am so sorry. I didn't even know that it was Reema I was kissing." His eyes shined in the sunlight that peeked through the window, and I told myself to turn away to avoid the urge to run into his arms. But it was also impossible not to stare into those amber beauties, especially when there was such sincerity in them.

"Calina, I thought it was you."

"What? That's the most ridiculous excuse I've heard." I rolled my eyes. Seriously? Did he really think that I would believe that?

"I know it sounds insane, but Reema came over to talk to me at halftime and she asked me some random question about chemistry. Then all of a sudden, the stadium was gone...and Reema disappeared. The next thing I knew, I was standing on a beach. And you were there...it was like I was in a dream, but it felt so real. You looked so beautiful, and the waves...I pulled you to me and kissed you." Oliver paused, still seemingly confused by the whole scenario, and pushed a hand through his thick hair. He looked at me, pleadingly. "I was kissing *you*. But I opened my eyes, and it wasn't you. There was no beach. Just the lacrosse field. And Reema."

I stood there in silence for a moment, trying to understand the crazy that he just spewed. Shani edged closer to me and put her hand on my shoulder.

"I think Reema used Chaos on him."

I remained silent and peered down at my shoes, more flowers sprouting up around me and tangling up the sides of our small dining table.

Oliver glanced down at the continuously blooming plants. "Sorry. Still working on the control thing, and I guess I'm still nervous." He half-smiled and his dimple appeared, melting my resolve to never forgive him.

He moved a few paces closer to me, carefully stepping over the new rose buds that were sprawling across the room. "Calina, I swear. I would never intentionally hurt you. And I have no interest in Reema. Please. You have to believe me." Suddenly, Oliver stopped short and grinned as if remembering something. He pointed to Shani and nearly shouted, "Shani read my mind! She saw what really happened. She'll tell you!"

"He's telling the truth. He was in another world. Well, another world in his mind, anyway." Shani stepped back towards her bedroom door as more and more flowers crawled over our dorm. "Oliver, can we maybe put a pause on the flower thing?"

Oliver glanced down again at the out-of-control plants surrounding us. "Yeah, I'm sorry...Let me try again." He closed his eyes in an intense concentration and the flowers stopped growing. He opened his eyes again and walked over to stand directly in front of me.

He warily took one of my hands in his and held it palm up. His brow rose in a silent question, and I relented, allowing him to hold my hand in place between us. He inched closer and gently let our foreheads rest on one another. I inhaled his warmth and closed my eyes, reveling in his touch.

Dammit.

"Open your eyes," he whispered, our heads still pressed together.

I opened my eyes and a tiny gardenia started to bloom right there in my hand, its luscious scent flooding my nostrils. Smiling, I turned my gaze from the flower to meet his eyes. They were that wondrous amber color as he stared at me, so intently.

"Please believe me. I was an idiot for falling for whatever it was that she did to me. I need you to forgive me."

"I do." I started to pull away, but he gripped my hand, holding me in place.

"Calina."

I melted each time he said my name. Blushing, I looked down at the gardenia, and his free hand took my chin, forcing me to meet his gaze once more.

"Calina, I love you."

I couldn't control the smile that formed on my lips. "I love you too."

Oliver let out a small exhale as if he'd been holding his breath while waiting for my response to his declaration. He let my hand, and the gardenia, fall and placed both of his hands on my cheeks, pressing his lips to mine. I wrapped my arms around his neck and fell into him, our lips moving in perfect unison.

"Eh-hem." Shani cleared her throat behind us. "Still standing here."

I reluctantly pulled myself away from Oliver's lips but kept my arms around his neck and turned my head to face Shani. Oliver rested his forehead on my temple, his hands firmly placed on my waist.

Shani appeared overly uncomfortable, and she made an effort to avert her eyes away from us. "I am super excited that you two are back together, but I think there is something else you need to discuss?" She finally made eye contact with Oliver. "Don't you have something you want to tell Cali?"

He loosened his grip on me and backed away, nearly tripping over a wisteria vine that had sprung up next to the roses. "Right. This is actually great news." Kicking off the vine from his heel, Oliver's eyes brightened. If that were even possible. "I am transferring. Here. To St. Anne's."

I beamed. His mother told me earlier that she thought it would be a good idea, but I wasn't sure if it was officially decided or not. "Oliver, that's amazing!" I went to throw my arms around him again and he held his hand up, making me pause.

"There's something else." Oliver gave a sidelong glance at Shani, and she stepped forward to stand beside him.

"Cali, Oliver's mom came by here looking for you. Instead, she found Oliver and told him that she was the one who shrouded his magic when he was a baby." Shani smiled wide at me and put a hand on Oliver's shoulder. "She undid her curse. So, now Oliver might have a fighting chance at learning to control his power."

I waited for the part about his father. About how dangerous undoing Oliver's curse might be if someone suspected that he was John Rowan's son. But the two of them just stared at me, waiting for my excitement, and smiling at the supposedly good news.

I guess I still had a secret to keep for now.

I cleared my throat and went to hug Oliver, indulging in the warmth of his arms and trying to ignore the tiny voice in the back of my head urging me to tell him everything I knew.

The voice was about to win, and I looked up at him prepared to spill my guts. "Oliver, I—"

His smile stopped me. He gazed back at me with pure happiness, and I couldn't take that from him. It wasn't my place.

He kissed my forehead. "What?"

I shook my head. "Nothing. I'm just excited that you'll be coming to the Academy." I rested my cheek on his chest silently cursing myself for being so weak.

I laughed seeing Shani's awkward expression as she backed away from us. I regrettably pulled away from Oliver's chest to give him a quick kiss, but he still kept his arms around my waist.

"I'm glad it all worked out...anyway, I'm going to study. Please remember that the walls are thin." Shani made a quick exit to her side of the dorm, and I was finally alone with Oliver.

His arms closed even tighter around me, if that was possible, and he whispered, "You know, with my affinity for starting fires and yours for biting, things could get a bit complicated." His lips brushed against my ear. "Or kinky."

I blushed against the heat rising throughout my body, a sly smile on my face. Then, reaching my arms up around his neck, I pulled his perfect face down to mine and pressed my lips to his. Oliver's kiss grew in intensity and, suddenly, he scooped me off the floor and carried me into my bedroom.

He tossed me gently on the comforter and fell onto me, his hands roaming along my side and hips and his lips finding mine. My eyes closed as his kiss traveled down my neck and along my collarbone and...

A loud pop sounded from Shani's room next to mine and I heard her yelp.

"Shit, my candle! Oliver!"

Oliver suddenly froze on top of me, mid kiss. "Sorry!" He called to the neighboring room, then looked down at me and we both started laughing before returning to our embrace.

With his hands around me, pulling me into him, I almost forgot about the challenges that we would face once he came to St. Anne's. There was a lot for us to figure out and this enormous secret was going to be nearly impossible to keep to myself.

But all of that would have to wait. Right now, the only thing that mattered was being in Oliver's arms and sharing that moment with him.

Oh, and remembering to buy a fire extinguisher.

About Jen Drapp

Jen Drapp writes fantasy and romance in the Adult and YA spaces. She survives off of Rockstar energy drinks and Netflix, and when she's not writing, she works as a Nursing Professor. She loves spending her free time reading, running, and travelling with her family and currently resides outside of Washington DC.

Follow her on social media:

www.jencdrapp.com

www.instagram.com/jencdrapp

www.facebook.com/authorjendrapp

www.tiktok.com/jencdrapp

www.ingramcontent.com/pod-product-compliance
Lightning Source LLC
Chambersburg PA
CBHW010428120726
47992CB00010B/3366